The
Black
Fawn

Other books by JIM KJELGAARD

THE LAND IS BRIGHT

THE LOST WAGON

BIG RED

REBEL SIEGE

FOREST PATROL

BUCKSKIN BRIGADE

CHIP, THE DAM BUILDER

FIRE HUNTER

IRISH RED

KALAK OF THE ICE

A NOSE FOR TROUBLE

SNOW DOG

TRAILING TROUBLE

WILD TREK

THE EXPLORATIONS OF PERE MARQUETTE

THE SPELL OF THE WHITE STURGEON

OUTLAW RED

THE COMING OF THE MORMONS

CRACKER BARREL TROUBLE SHOOTER

LION HOUND

TRADING JEFF AND HIS DOG

DESERT DOG

HAUNT FOX

THE OKLAHOMA LAND RUN

DOUBLE CHALLENGE

SWAMP CAT

WILDLIFE CAMERAMAN

WOLF BROTHER

RESCUE DOG OF THE HIGH PASS

The
Black
Fawn

by Jim Kjelgaard

Dodd, Mead & Company

New York

The
Black
Fawn

chapter   1

EVENING SHADOWS LOW-
ered like a cool, dark wing folding gently over the day,
but the coming of night brought no change in the refrain that over and over again kept running through
Bud Sloan's brain.

"I must not let them know I'm afraid. I must remember my manners. I must not let them know I'm
afraid! I must remember my manners! I must not . . ."

He clenched his teeth as though somehow that
would clamp down on the unwanted words and shove
them back into the dark recesses where they belonged.

But they were in his brain, not his mouth, and clenching his teeth only seemed to make the refrain ring all the more loudly. He opened his mouth and said before he could stop himself,

"I must not . . ."

"You must not what?" Gram Bennett asked.

She sat at the side of the little table in the kitchen and not at the great one in the dining room as when all the Bennetts' eleven children were home. Then Gramps sat at the head of the table and Gram at the foot. But the little table was big enough now that there were only three of them for most meals.

"Nothing." Bud choked. "I—I was just thinking out loud."

"You needn't be afraid to speak up, Allan. If there's something you must not do, you have only to say so."

Gram spoke very gently, but Bud squirmed. He did not wriggle on his chair for he had learned to hide as well as he could what he really felt. To show your feelings was to show your weakness, and there was always somebody ready to pounce on a weakness. He should have known better than to talk out loud.

"Tell us, Allan," Gram coaxed.

"There's nothing to tell," he said, looking down at his plate and feeling his cheeks flush.

He HAD COME TO LIVE WITH GRAM AND GRAMPS only yesterday morning and it seemed an eternity since the bus driver had stopped on the blacktop road and pointed out the rutted drive leading to the Bennetts' huge old farmhouse.

"That's it, son," he had said.

With his little bundle of belongings wrapped in a spare shirt and tucked under his right arm—the orphanage did not furnish suitcases when they farmed you out—Bud started up the drive with his head high and with what he hoped was a fearless, manly tread. But his insides felt like jelly that has stood too long in a warm place and his feet seemed to weigh five hundred pounds each. If he had been sure no one was looking, he would have burst into tears. He could not be sure, and not for an instant must he forget that weakness made him an easy prey for whoever saw it. He did not think of running.

Bud was twenty yards from the house when Gramps Bennett came around one corner. Bud stopped in his tracks and grasped his bundle so tightly that his knuckles whitened.

At first glance Gramps seemed to be a huge man, but after a second look you saw that he merely seemed huge because he was short. He stood five feet six in

3

his work-scuffed brogans, faded blue jeans and an equally faded denim work shirt. He seemed to be almost as big around as he was tall. Hamlike hands hung from his shirt sleeves, a short, thick neck rose from the collar. A stubby white beard almost hid Gramps' lips and he had an aquiline nose, piercing eyes and a leonine mane of white hair. Gramps' voice sounded like a lion's roar as he said,

"You the boy from the orphanage?"

"Yes, sir," Bud said, still trying to conduct himself as a man should.

"Got a name?" Gramps asked caustically.

"Yes, sir," the boy said. "Bud Sloan."

"Bud, eh? I've heard worse names. Come meet Gram."

Without another word or a backward look and with astonishing agility for his bulk, Gramps turned on his heel and led the way to the kitchen door at the back of the house. There was also a front door, but that was for company use.

Bud felt better when he saw four cattle in a pasture near the barn. Two horses raised inquiring heads over the bars of the paddock, pigs grunted in their sty and chickens, ducks and turkeys roamed at will around the farmyard. Then a big and furry farm collie came trot-

4

ting slowly toward the house.

Bud almost smiled. He had always understood animals. He did not know why, unless it was because they always accepted him for what he was and never cared where he came from or who supported him. His most cherished memory of the orphanage was a pet kitten he had had there. His first heartbreak had come when that kitten had been killed by a passing car. Seeing the animals here seemed somehow to remove half his burdens.

Bud turned for a last look at the dog before Gramps opened the door and he entered the kitchen to meet Gram.

"Why, Allan! How wonderful you're here at last!"

Bud writhed. For although his proper name was Allan, he hated it.

Gram was taller than Gramps, and slim. Her hair was gray. Sixty years and eleven children had left their mark on her face and work-worn hands, but her tread was lithe and easy as she advanced on Bud. When she stooped to enfold him in her arms, she seemed taller than the Eiffel Tower. Gram planted a resounding kiss on his cheek.

"Welcome, Allan, and may you be happy with us!"

Bud sputtered and squirmed away from Gram. It

was the first time he could remember being kissed and he considered it a degrading experience. He looked up to see Gramps regarding him balefully.

"You told me your name was Bud," Gramps snorted.

"It is!"

"Pooh," said Gram. "It's Allan written on the card and it's Allan I'll call him. Have a tart, Allan."

She gave him a crisp-baked tart filled with jelly. Bud meant to refuse it, for he neither asked for nor wanted favors. But a boy's hunger asserted itself and he accepted it, mumbled his thanks and began to eat it, looking around the kitchen as he did.

He noticed only that it was much smaller than the kitchen at the orphanage and that the huge, old-fashioned wood-burning range, the wooden cupboards, the pantry off the kitchen and the worn furniture and scuffed linoleum looked shabby in comparison with the antiseptic, modern appointments of the orphanage kitchen.

Bud finished the tart and, stealing a glance into the adjoining living room, saw a mounted buck's head peering glassily back at him. Hastily he wiped his hands on his trousers and looked away.

"Do you think you'll like it here?" Gram asked.

"Yes, ma'am," Bud said dutifully.

"Will you have another tart?"

"No, ma'am."

"Yes, ma'am. No, ma'am," Gramps mimicked. "That all they taught you to say at that there orphanage?"

"No, sir."

"Well, if you've had all you want to eat, Bud," Gramps said, looking meaningfully at Gram as he emphasized the nickname, "we might as well put you to work."

"Now, Delbert," Gram said, "I say that boy ought to rest his first day with us."

"And I say he ought not," Gramps said firmly. "He might as well get the idea why he's here from the first, and why he's here is to work. Come on, Bud."

Bud said nothing as he turned to follow Gramps out of the kitchen, but he was not worried. He had known he was coming to work. Tales from other farmed-out youngsters had drifted back to the orphanage and some of them were not pretty tales, but anything was better than continuing as an object of charity. He was a man and he could stand on his own two feet. Although he might not like what came, he could face it.

He felt a little better when they came onto the back porch. The big dog that had been ambling toward the house when he arrived was now lying on the stoop. It rose, wagged its tail amiably and touched Bud's hand with a moist muzzle. No matter what happened, Bud thought, it couldn't be all bad now that he had a friend.

Gramps did not stop or look back until they came to a broad cultivated field in which orderly rows of fledgling crops had been so carefully planted and so precisely spaced that they formed an exact pattern. The dog, who knew that he was not to walk on cultivated ground, sat down at the edge of the field. Bud asked his name.

"Shep," Gramps said, and then he pointed to the field. "Do you know what those are?"

"No, sir."

"Beans," said Gramps, and the tone of his voice showed pity for anybody unable to identify a growing bean. "Now stoop down here 'longside me."

Bud did as he was told and Gramps caught a bean, which had broad leaves and a fragile stem, between his forefingers and held it gently.

"Have yourself a real good look."

Bud concentrated on the bean until a full minute later when Gramps said,

"Know what it looks like?"

"Yes, sir."

"Good. Now, everything in this field that ain't a bean

is a weed. Every weed steals from the beans just like a bank robber steals from a bank."

"I don't understand you, sir," Bud said.

"Think, boy, and quit calling me sir," Gramps said impatiently. "What makes the beans grow big and strong, if not the goodness of the earth? And what else do the weeds live on? For every weed that steals the earth's richness, the beans suffer accordingly."

"That's wonderful!"

Gramps looked at him oddly, but Bud was too surprised and delighted to notice. He had never thought of nature in such terms and it *was* wonderful. Gramps got down on his hands and knees and, supporting himself on both knees and with his left hand, deftly used his right hand to pluck a small weed from among the growing beans. He held the weed up for Bud to look at.

"There you are. A pigweed, and a month from now it would be waist high to you. Its roots would be so big and grown so deep that when you pulled it out a half dozen beans would come with it. Now, between the rows we can hoe 'em out or cultivate 'em. But we can't use either a hoe or cultivator on the rows themselves, and I guess even you can see why."

"Yes, sir."

Gramps' tone remained caustic but Bud refused to

be ruffled. He would earn his own way and the right to hold his head high.

"Sure you know what a bean looks like?" Gramps asked.

"Yes, sir."

"Then I want you to work down all these rows and pick the weeds out from the beans."

Bud got down on his hands and knees and started on the first row. He was more interested than he had thought he could be, for what otherwise would have been an onerous task took on new meaning in the light of what Gramps had told him. He was not just pulling weeds; he was destroying robbers bent on stealing for themselves the goodness from the earth that properly belonged to the growing beans.

When he thought he was surely at the end of the row, he looked up to find that he was less than halfway down it. Then another sight caught his eyes.

Beyond the barn and the pasture, where the cattle now stood lazily in the shade of a single tree and chewed placid cuds, the unbroken green border of the forest began. The trees were cutover hardwoods for the most part, but here and there a pine rose above them and an occasional gaunt stub towered over even the pines. Bud looked and wondered and promised himself that, as soon as he could, he would go into the forest and see for himself what was there. But now there were weeds to pull.

After what seemed an eternity, he reached the end of the first row and turned back on the second one. He did not look up again, for he felt guilty about stopping work. He tried to forget the ache in his bent back and the strain on his legs, for he knew he must work. When at last he came to the end of the second row and turned back on the third, he heard Gram saying,

"I've brought you a drink, Allan. Real, honest-to-goodness ice-cold lemonade. Come have some."

Bud rose to his knees, trying hard not to wince, and saw Gram, who was wearing a faded gingham dress and a sunbonnet that had gone out of style a quarter of a century ago. She was carrying a pail from which the handle of a tin dipper protruded and in which chunks of ice tinkled. Cold droplets clung to the outer surface of the pail.

Gram smiled as Bud came forward, and he looked at her warily. There was no telling what might happen when people smiled. But thirst triumphed over caution. He filled the dipper, drained it, and filled it and drained it again. Ice-cold lemonade was delicious in any case and it seemed twenty times better from a tin dipper.

"More?" Gram said.

"No thank you, ma'am."

"How is it going?"

"Very well, ma'am."

"Don't you work too hard," she said, and went off to offer some lemonade to Gramps.

Bud went back to his weeding, crawling slowly along the lines of beans with his eyes fixed on their lower stalks. Anything that was not a bean must be a weed, Gramps had said, and Bud acted accordingly. By now the romance of what he was doing had faded, but he kept on, determined to pay his own way.

A sudden bellow from Gramps was as startling as the wail of a fire engine. "Hey, Bud. Don'cha eat at noon?"

Bud rose and turned to face the old man, who said, "Don't the sun tell you it's noon?"

"No," Bud said.

"When the sun's where she is, and when she don't

cast 'nough shadow to hide a grasshopper, it's noon."

Bud pondered this new and fascinating bit of lore. He looked at the sun and tried to fix its position indelibly in his mind so that forever afterward he would know when it was noon. Though the sun had never told him anything before, from now on it would.

"Let's move!" Gramps bellowed.

Bud followed. Shep, who had devoted the cool portion of the morning to sniffing out various creatures in their lairs and had then gone to lie in the tall grass when the sun became hot, joined them. Bud and Gramps washed at the old hand pump beside the stoop, rubbed their hands and faces dry with a rough towel that hung over the pump and went into the kitchen.

Bud sank wearily into his chair and it seemed to him that he had never before known how good it could be just to sit down. But he had worked too hard not to be even hungrier than usual, and he could not ignore the smell of the food on the table.

Gram's lunch began with pork chops and mashed potatoes and ended with a delicious chilled product of the kitchen's major concession to modern living, a big refrigerator.

There was no time for conversation or anything else

except eating. Gramps emptied his plate first, pushed it back and sighed contentedly. A moment later when Bud had drained his final glass of milk, Gramps said,

"How about getting back to work?"

"Yes, sir."

"Delbert," Gram said sharply, "that boy should rest."

"Pshaw. He'll rest better after he works harder. How 'bout it?"

"Yes, sir," Bud said without enthusiasm.

The morning had been hard and the afternoon was torture. But Bud stayed grimly with the weeds until the sun lowered and Gramps called to him that it was time for supper. Bud was almost reeling with fatigue and he was grateful when Gramps pumped a basin of water for him to wash in. Although he happily stuffed himself with Gram's supper, only his resolution to show no weakness kept him from dozing once supper was over.

Evidently as brisk as he had been in the early morning, Gramps bounced from his chair. "If you're done, Bud, how 'bout giving me a hand with the milking?"

"Delbert," Gram said, "you're a . . ."

"I'm a what?" Gramps asked innocently.

"A Simon Legree. You're working that youngster a sight harder than you ever worked yourself."

Gramps said piously, "The Lord said there shall be a day and there shall be a night. Man shall work for as long as day shall last. Right offhand, I can't rightly recall if He said anything 'bout working nights, but I expect He didn't know much about farmers or He would have. Anyhow, those cows got to be milked."

"Until now you've managed very nicely to milk them yourself."

"But now I got a boy to help me with all the chores I used to do," Gramps said. "C'mon, Bud."

Bud trailed the old man to the barn where Gramps flicked on the switch that lighted it. The first thing Bud noticed was the barn's odor, pungent and sweet, with only a faint suggestion of rancidness.

Locked in their stanchions, the four cows were either nibbling grain from the boxes that stood beside each of them or lustily chewing hay. Bud stood back. Pulling weeds had been strange enough. The cows in their stanchions were as alien as visitors from another planet.

Gramps went to the end of the stable, opened a small door and disappeared through it. He returned with two milking pails. He kept one and thrust the other at Bud, who took it although he hadn't the faintest notion of what he was supposed to do with it.

"Ever do any milking?" Gramps demanded.

15

"No, sir."

"You'll never learn any younger. I'll show you."

He pulled a stool up beside a placid red and white cow that was so used to being milked that she did not even move when Gramps began to strip her udders. It looked easy. But when Gramps rose and motioned for Bud to take his place, the best Bud could do was to coax a trickle from one teat and a few drops from another. Gramps watched for a moment without comment and went to milk another cow.

Bud continued the uneven struggle but there was less than an inch of milk in the bottom of the pail when Gramps returned. He watched a moment and said,

"Let me do it."

Bud was thankful, but he tried hard not to show that he was as he surrendered the milking stool and let Gramps sit down. Milk hissed and foamed into the pail as Gramps took every last drop of milk from the cow's swollen udders. Bud went with him to the little room at the end of the stable and, feeling guilty and ashamed, watched him pour the milk into a can that stood neck-deep in cold water.

Back in the house he fell asleep as soon as his head struck the pillow. He was too tired to notice the room or anything except that he was in bed.

He seemed scarcely to have fallen asleep when he felt someone shaking him awake. Bud opened his eyes to see the murky dawn at the windows and Gramps standing over him.

"Come on," Gramps said. "We don't lay abed on farms."

Bud waited until Gramps had gone, for now that he was awake, it didn't seem possible that he could hurt in so many places and all at the same time. Then he climbed stiffly out of bed and dressed. When he walked downstairs to breakfast, his head was high and his step was as firm as he could make it.

The second day was a repetition of the first, except that when the beans were finished, Gramps set him to weeding onions. But more and more often Bud raised his head to look at the surrounding forest, and he renewed his promise to himself to find out what lay behind those trees at the edge of the forest.

BUD LOOKED RESENTFULLY DOWN AT HIS EMPTY PIE plate and, as much as he wanted to, he could not look up again.

"I guess," Gram said, "that a body needn't tell all he knows and is a fool if he does. Whatever it is you mustn't do, don't do it. I'm sure Delbert will do the milking tonight. Why don't you go for a walk in the woods?"

He sprang up with renewed energy and went outside. Shep rose to tag along with him and together they entered the cool forest.

Bud walked slowly. He did not know how to interpret the things he saw and heard around him, but he did not doubt that all of it was wonderful. He jumped when an owl cried, was frightened for a moment when a dead snag crashed with an unearthly noise and laughed when a jay shrieked. His confidence mounted so that when he heard two sharp, blasting snorts, he continued to advance.

Two minutes later he stopped in his tracks. Not twenty feet away, its wobbly feet braced to keep it from falling, a tiny fawn no more than two hours old stared at him in wide-eyed wonder.

chapter 2

THE FAWN TREMBLED ON
legs so new and untried, and so slender that they
seemed scarcely able to support his jack-rabbit-sized
body. His ears were ridiculously long and his staring,
fascinated eyes were all out of proportion to his tiny
head. The white stripes and spots that mark the young
of all white-tailed deer stood out against an undercoat-
ing of hair that was abnormally dark; on the neck and
shoulders it was nearly black.

The gentle Shep wagged his tail and took a step
nearer this tiny wild baby. Raising a front foot, the

fawn tapped a hoof no bigger than a twenty-five-cent piece and looked back over his shoulder at the laurel copse where the doe had left him. Scenting the approach of a dog and a human being, she had fled. The little buck should have stayed in hiding, but his natural curiosity had overridden the doe's warning not to move.

For a moment Bud was too bewildered and delighted to think clearly. Then he was lifted on a cloud of ecstasy and sympathy. He was sure the fawn had been abandoned by his father and mother or that they were dead. Like Bud, the little buck was left to shift for himself in a cheerless and friendless world, and Bud felt that he was forever bound to this tiny deer. There was a bond between them that nothing else could share and nothing could ever break. As long as either endured, Bud decided, each would love the other because each understood the other. They were brothers.

"Hi, little guy," Bud said softly.

Shep, tail wagging, head bent and ears tumbled forward, stayed beside him as he took the fawn in both arms. Soft as a cloud, the fawn surrendered to his embrace and gravely smelled his arm with a nose as delicate as an orchid.

"Don't be afraid," Bud crooned. "You won't be hurt. Nothing will ever hurt you."

He spoke almost fiercely, mindful of his own many hurts, and stared into space as he cradled the fawn. Shep sat near, his jaws parted and beaming approval as only a dog can. Bud's heart spiraled upward. Now, at last, he had found a true friend.

He was unaware of passing time or of long evening shadows. He only knew that he wanted to stay with this little black buck forever.

"WHAT'D YOU FIND, BUD?"

Bud had not heard Gramps Bennett come up behind him. A terrible vision of the glass-eyed buck's head in the farm living room arose in Bud's mind and he looked about wildly for a place in which to hide the fawn. But it was too late to hide it, and he turned slowly, so as not to startle the little buck, and said truculently,

"Shep found this little lost deer."

"Well, now," Gramps said, ignoring Bud's belligerent tone, "doggone if he didn't. Cute little feller, too, and he's sure taken a shine to you."

Gramps stooped beside the pair and stroked the fawn

softly. Bud stared at him, for Gramps was no longer the tyrant who acted as if Bud were a machine for getting beans weeded and cows milked.

"Its . . . Its . . . ," Bud tried to get out.

And then he could not explain. How could he describe all the terror, all the loneliness and all the fear that he had felt to one who had never known these things? Bud gritted his teeth and looked stubbornly away.

"Its what?" Gramps asked.

"Its father and mother have run away and left it," Bud blurted out.

"Let me put you straight on that, Bud. Its mother ran away when she smelled or saw you and Shep coming. Fathers of baby deer like this, well, they just don't care much for their young 'uns."

Bud was astonished. "You mean it had no father?"

Gramps said solemnly, "I haven't seen any fawn-carrying storks round here for might' nigh two years. This baby had a father all right, maybe Old Yellowfoot himself."

"Who's Old Yellowfoot?"

"If you'd been round here for two months 'stead of just a couple days, you'd never ask that," Gramps said. "Old Yellowfoot's nothing 'cept the biggest and smartest buck ever left a hoofprint in Bennett's Woods or, as far as that goes, in Dishnoe County. Why, Boy, Old Yellowfoot's got a rack of antlers the like of which even I never saw, and I've been hunting deer in these parts for, let's see, it's lacking two of fifty years."

"You . . ." Bud hugged the fawn a little tighter. "You shoot the deer?"

Gramps said seriously, "You look at that fawn, then you look at me, and you ask in the same tone you might use if you thought I was going to murder some babies, 'You shoot the deer?' Well, I don't shoot the deer. I could, mind you, 'cause next to lacing your own shoes, just about the easiest thing round here is shooting a deer. But I don't even hunt the deer. I hunt Old Yellowfoot and some day, so help me, his head'll hang 'longside the one you saw in the sitting room."

"I could never like it!" Bud said.

Gramps remained serious. "You say that, but you don't know what you're talking 'bout 'cause you never tried it. You see this baby and he sure is cute as a button —he's going to be a black buck when he grows up—but right now he hasn't the sense of a half-witted mud turtle. That's not to be wondered at. He hasn't had time to learn sense and, if he had any, he wouldn't let you handle him like he was a puppy. You think he's so pretty, so nice, so friendly, and you're right. You think also he's a deer, and he sure is. You go astray when you think anybody who'd shoot this fawn, a deer, is more brute than human and you're partly right. But, Boy, there's as much difference 'twixt this baby and Old Yellowfoot as there is between a sparrow and an ostrich!"

Interested in spite of himself, Bud asked, "What's the difference?"

"The difference? Old Yellowfoot ain't as smart as the men that hunt him. He's a darn' sight smarter. Hunt him high and hunt him low, and if you get one look at him, in cover too thick for shooting or so far off that it's useless to shoot, you can call yourself a hunter. Hang his head on the wall and you're in a class with the best. Old Yellowfoot's educated and he got his education the hard way. Hunters gave it to him. For the past five years, fifty hunters I know of have had him marked. Nobody's brought him in, and that says enough. But maybe, come deer season, you and me will nail him. What say?"

Bud stirred uneasily, for this was something new to him. In every crisis of his life he had found the love and affection he craved in animals. It was unthinkable to hurt, let alone to kill, a bird or beast. He asked finally,

24

"How long have you been hunting Old Yellowfoot?"

"Ever since he's sported the biggest rack of antlers of any buck I know. That's five years."

Bud breathed a little easier. Gramps had hunted the big buck for five years; it was highly unlikely that he would kill him the sixth year. When Bud remained silent, Gramps asked again,

"What say? When the season rolls round, are you and me going to hunt Old Yellowfoot?"

Bud said reluctantly, "I'll go with you. I'll carry your gun."

"Pooh!" Gramps snorted. "In the first place it ain't a gun. It's a rifle. What's more, you'll be carrying your own. Seven boys and four girls Mother and me raised on this farm. Every one hunted, and when they left the farm, they left their rifles and shotguns. One of 'em's sure to suit you."

Bud thought of a beautiful dapple-gray toy horse with a real leather saddle and bridle that he had seen in a store window when he had been six. He had wanted that horse more than he had ever wanted anything and every night he had prayed for it. But after his birthday had come and gone and his letters to Santa Claus been unavailing, he had concluded that dreams never come true and from then on had stifled his desires.

Now, listening to Gramps, Bud wanted a gun of his own more than he had wanted anything since the dapple-gray toy horse. He was not sure just what he would do with a rifle, except that he would never kill anything, but that did not lessen the glory of having one of his own like Daniel Boone, Jedediah Smith, Kit Carson, Buffalo Bill and a host of other heroes.

"Gosh," Bud said at last.

"I know what you mean," Gramps said, "and it's time we were getting back. Mother will fret if we're away too long."

Bud stooped and gathered the black fawn in his arms. It was as wispy as it looked and seemed to have no weight as it snuggled contentedly against him.

Gramps said, "We'll leave him, Bud."

"Leave him?"

It was a cry of anguish. The thought of abandoning the little buck, already once abandoned, was unbearable. He had forged a true bond with another living creature that had nobody except him. He couldn't leave it.

"We'll leave him," Gramps repeated firmly. "He belongs in the woods."

"Hunters will kill him!"

Gramps smiled. "Come deer season, that little guy

won't have aught except buttons. Next year he'll be a spike—that's a buck with no tines on his antlers—or maybe a forkhorn—that's a buck with one tine. He's safe for a while. If he's smart and lucky, maybe he's safe for a long while."

"He'll die with no one to look after him!"

"He has somebody to look after him. Maybe his pappy don't pay him any heed but, though she run off and left him when you and Shep came, his mammy sure thinks a heap of her son. There are those who say she'll never come back now that he's been handled and has human scent on him. If ever they say that to you, you tell 'em, 'Hogwash.' She'll be back."

Bud hesitated. All his life he had searched for something, and now that he had found the fawn, he was being asked to leave it. Rebellion mounted within him.

"On second thought," Gramps said disinterestedly, "fetch him along if you've a mind to. His mammy'll be sorehearted for a time when she comes back for him and he ain't here, but she'll get over it."

Bud gasped. The mother he had never known was a hundred different people, most of them imaginary. He had never known exactly what she was like, or even what he wanted her to be like. But if he ever found her, he knew how she would feel if he were taken away.

"We'll leave him," he said.

He put the fawn down, and the little black buck minced a few steps and jerked his tail playfully. As he watched, Bud knew that the bond between him and the fawn would remain. They were blood brothers even if their form and species were different.

Reluctantly he fell in beside Gramps and, with Shep tagging at their heels, they started back toward the farmhouse. Bud turned to look again at the fawn. He thought he saw the doe emerge from a thicket and return to her lost baby, but he realized at once that he was imagining what he wanted to see. Then they rounded a bend and the next time Bud looked back he could not see the fawn at all. He stifled an almost overpowering urge to run back to the fawn.

"His mother will really come back to care for him?" he asked Gramps.

"Don't you fret, she'll come back and like as not she's there now. Do you like to fish for trout, Bud?"

"I don't know. I've never tried it."

"What did you fish for?"

"Nothing. I just never fished."

"Imagine that," Gramps said happily. "You'll start, with me tomorrow morning. I'll show you the biggest gosh-darned brown trout as ever sucked a fly off Skunk

Crick, and ain't that a heck of a name for a crick? But this trout, he's named right good. Old Shark, they call him, and he's busted enough leaders and rods to stock a good-sized tackle store. Wait'll you see him."

The way Gramps spoke of Old Yellowfoot, the great buck, and Old Shark, the great trout, drove the black fawn from Bud's thoughts. He fought against it, but he could not help a warm feeling toward this man who spoke of wild creatures, or at least of mighty wild creatures with near reverence and who believed that, if you were going to kill, or try to kill them, you should pit yourself against a worthy opponent.

What had happened to the old farmer who had seemed able to think only of starting the day at dawn with milking his four cows and of ending it after dark with milking the same cows? Then Bud's conscience smote him.

"We can't fish tomorrow!"

"And why not?"

"I came here to work."

Gramps said dryly, "The work is always with us, and sometimes it seems like Old Shark's always been with us, too. But while the work won't end, Old Shark will if I lay another fly into him. Or maybe you'll do it?"

Bud started to speak and stopped. Many a time during his years in the orphanage he had watched prospective parents come and go, and he had yearned to go with some of them. Then, along with most of the others who had passed the age of seven without being adopted, he had finally realized that nobody wanted him. Nor would anybody want him until he was old enough to work. And if he did not work, how could he justify his existence?

"What were you going to say?" Gramps asked.

"I'm not afraid to work."

" 'Course you ain't. Nobody worth his salt is afraid to work, but there's a time for work and," Gramps paused as if for emphasis, "there's a time for fishing. Tomorrow we'll milk the cows, turn 'em out to pasture, and go fishing."

"Yes, sir."

"Call me Gramps," Gramps said.

"Yes, Gramps," Bud said warily. He was bewildered by the idea of going fishing when he should be working. Where was the trap, he wondered?

They came to the house, went around to the kitchen door, and Shep went to his bed on the back porch. The kitchen was brightly lighted, and Bud thought he saw Gram back hastily away from the door, as though she had been watching for them. But when they entered,

30

Gram was sitting at the table knitting. Near her, at Bud's place, was a tall glass of cold milk and a huge cut of strawberry pie. Gram looked over her glasses and frowned at Bud but she spoke to Gramps.

"Delbert, you were a long while bringing Allan back."

"Now, Mother," he said, "it's been nigh onto fourteen years since anybody saw a man-eating lion in Bennett's Woods."

"Hmph!" Gram snorted. "It might not be so funny if that boy had strayed into the woods and got lost."

"But he didn't get lost," Gramps said reasonably. "Bud and me, we met out in the woods and had us a good long talk."

Something in Gramps' voice turned Gram's frown into a smile.

"Well, you're both here now and I suppose that's what matters. Allan, sit down and eat your pie and drink your milk."

"I'm really not hungry," Bud protested.

"Pooh! All boys are hungry all the time. Sit down and eat."

"Yes, ma'am."

He sat down, took a long drink of the cold milk, ate a fork full of pie and found that he was hungry after all. Looking around Gram's kitchen as he ate, he thought of the one at the orphanage where, in spite of the thousands of dishes he had wiped there and the bushels of potatoes he had peeled, he had never been invited to sit down to a glass of cold milk and a cut of pie. It was a very disquieting thing, and his wariness mounted. He looked furtively around again for a trap, but Gram had returned to her knitting and Gramps was delving into a leather-covered case.

Gramps' case was a homemade thing divided into a number of small compartments. One by one, he took from their respective compartments an assortment of varicolored objects and arranged them on a piece of newspaper. They looked like insects but were made from tiny bits of feathers and wisps of hair. Each one was arranged about a hook. The biggest was not large and the smallest was so tiny and so fragile that it looked as if the merest puff of wind would whirl it away. Bud looked on agog.

"Dry flies," Gramps said. "I don't know what he'll take, but we'll try him first with a black gnat."

"Yes, sir."

"Call me Gramps," the old man growled.

"Yes, Gramps."

This time it slipped out, naturally and easily, almost

warmly, for the flies were so interesting that Bud forgot everything else. Although he had never been fishing, he had always believed that you fished with a stout pole, a strong hank of line, a hook and worms for bait. But these dry flies were plainly conceived by one artist and tied by another. It was easy to see that only an artist could use them properly. Gramps took one of the smaller ones between his thumb and forefinger, and the fly seemed even smaller in comparison with the hand holding it.

"Yup, I think a number-fourteen black gnat is what he'll hit, which proves all over again what a dam' old fool I am. Saying aforehand what Old Shark will hit is like saying it will rain on the seventh of May two years from now. Might and might not, and the chances are three hundred and sixty-four to one it won't. Have a look, Bud."

Bud took the delicate mite in his own hand and held it gingerly. The longer he looked, the more wonderful it seemed.

"Where do you get them?" he asked.

"I tie 'em. Got good and tired of using store-bought flies that won't take anything 'cept baby trout or those just out of a hatchery that haven't any sense. Let's see it, Bud."

Gramps returned the fly to its proper place and Bud was half glad and half sorry to give it up. He was afraid he might damage the fly, but at the same time he yearned to examine it at length. He stole a glance at Gramps' huge hands and marvelled. It was easy to believe that those hands could guide a plow, shoe a horse, fit a hoe and do almost any job that demanded sheer strength. But it seemed incredible that they could assemble with such perfection anything as minute and fragile as a dry fly.

Suddenly, and surprisingly, for he was no more aware of being tired than he had been of being hungry, Bud yawned. Gram looked up.

"You'd best get to bed, Allan. Growing boys need their rest as much as they do their food."

"Good idea, Bud," Gramps said. "If you and me are going to get the milking done and hit Skunk Crick when we ought, we'll have to roll out early."

Bud said good night and went up the worn stairs to his room. For a moment he stared out of the window into the night, yearning toward the little black buck and worrying about how it was faring. It seemed impossible for anything so small and helpless to survive. But he was not as desperately worried as he had been, for Gramps had said that the doe would return to take care of it. And Bud knew that in Gramps he had at last found somebody he could trust.

Leaving his bedroom door open to take advantage of a cool breeze blowing through the window, Bud stretched luxuriously on the feather-filled mattress and pulled the blankets up to his chin. Gram's voice came up the stairway.

"Well, Delbert?"

"He came round," he heard Gramps say. "He came round lot sooner'n I figured. Found himself a fawn, he did, cutest little widget you ever laid eyes on and almost black." There was a short silence and Gramps finished, "He thought it was 'nother orphan."

"So?"

"So tomorrow morning Bud and me are going to fish for Old Shark."

"How will he tie that in with being worked like a Mexican slave his first two days with us?"

Gramps said, "You take a skittish, scared colt out of pasture and put it to work, you work it hard enough so it forgets about being skittish and scared. And Mexicans aren't slaves, Mother."

"You, Delbert!"

"It worked," Gramps said.

Gram sniffed, "So'd Allan, and no wonder. You

wouldn't go down and pick a boy, as any sensible man would have done. You wrote a letter saying we'll give bed, board and schooling to a strong, healthy boy who's capable of working. Send the boy! I hope Allan didn't see that letter!"

"It's no mind if he did, and why do you suppose I wrote in 'stead of going in? Think I wanted that horse-faced old bat who runs the place to have fits?"

"Miss Dempster is not a horse-faced old bat!" Gram said sharply.

"She'd still have fits if she had to figure out anything not written down in her rule book, and it says in her book that older orphans are for working only. Anyway what does it matter? Ain't we got a young'un round the place again?"

"Yes!" Gram sighed. "Thank Heaven!"

Bud heard the last of this conversation only dimly, for sleep was overcoming him. He was even more vaguely aware of someone ascending the stairs, pausing beside his bed and planting a kiss on his cheek. Then he was lost in a happy dream of a mother who loved and cherished him and whom he loved and cherished.

chapter 3

THE OIL LANTERN THAT
hung from a hook in the ceiling of the cow stable cast
a progressively weaker glow as the light of a summer
dawn became stronger. Bud sat on a milking stool, his
head pillowed against the soft flank of the same red and
white cow that he had tried so hard, and so futilely, to
milk when he had first come to live with Gram and
Gramps Bennett.

Milk did not surge into the pail as it did when
Gramps milked; Gramps milked a cow almost as
though the animal's teats were spigots that he could

turn on at will and with no effort on his part. But there was no comparison between this and Bud's first sorry attempt to coax milk from the same cow. Her name was Susie, and when he gave her an affectionate pat she turned and looked at him with mournful eyes.

As Bud began to strip the last few squirts from each teat, he thought about the day ahead. He had slept soundly and the dawn had been so faint that his bedroom window was almost black when Gramps had awakened him. Bud had sat up hastily and a bit guiltily. His dream of a mother was still with him and in that uncertain moment between sleep and wakefulness, he half believed the dream was real.

Gramps had said, "Time to get under way, Bud," and then left.

Bud had dressed and gone at once to the window to stare toward the place where he had left the black fawn. As he stood there, he had heard a thousand faint scrapings, rustlings and murmurings of an entire world that seemed anxious to greet a new day, and he had whirled around to go down the stairs, through the empty kitchen and on out to the cow barn. He was coaxing a final trickle of milk from Susie when Gramps said,

"Let me have your pail and turn 'em out, will you?"

Bud wondered again that a man of Gramps' age and bulk could move so stealthily. Bud had not known Gramps had been beside him in the woods last night until the old man had spoken, and now Gramps had surprised him again. Bud surrendered his pail proudly for this was the first time he had been able to milk one cow while Gramps was milking three. Then he freed the cows from their stanchions and walked behind them as they lumbered out the open barn door and down the lane to the pasture.

"See you at the house," Gramps bellowed.

By the time Bud came into the kitchen, Gram had transformed it from the empty, silent and forbidding room it had been when he had walked through it earlier. Now the big stove cast a warm glow, hotcakes were browning on a griddle, bacon sizzled in a skillet, the coffeepot steamed and Bud's milk was poured. Gram glanced up and the corners of her eyes crinkled.

"My land, Allan. It's really going to be a big day."

"Yes, ma'am," he said stiffly.

Her smile became wistful and Bud flushed and looked away. It was easy to fight back when the enemy had a ferocious scowl and charged with clenched fists. It was hard when the weapons were glasses of cold milk and big wedges of pie, smiles, tender glances and soft words, and when the enemy seemed to know exactly what you were thinking. But Bud had no intention of letting himself be deceived.

Gramps, who was nowhere in sight when Bud entered the kitchen, appeared presently with a jointed fly rod that had a reel attached to the reel seat.

"Try this on for size," he said.

He placed the butt end of the rod in Bud's hand, and the boy tightened his fingers around the cork grip. The tip swayed downward. When Bud jerked it up, it collided with a chair and the rod bent in an arc before he could swing it away. Bud stood there frightened, not knowing what to do and not daring to move. The rod undulated and quivered like a live thing that had a mind and a will of its own. It seemed to defy control.

"It ain't a club," Gramps said. "Don't grab it like one. Let me show you."

He took the rod from Bud. Tensed like a hunting cat about to pounce, the rod still seemed to have a life of its own. But it had surrendered its will to Gramps. He was master of this delicate rod just as he was master of so many things, and Bud could not help admiring.

"I'll string her up and let you try her out."

"Not in my kitchen you won't," Gram said firmly. "I'll have no more dishes broken by practice casts."

On the point of arguing, Gramps reconsidered and said meekly, "I'll show you when we get on the crick. Take her and hold her this way."

He put the rod back in Bud's hand, placing it with Bud's palm just back of the seated reel and arranging his thumb and each finger for proper balance. Bud remained afraid to move it, or to shift even one finger, for now he commanded the rod. If he made one wrong move, and any move he made might be wrong, the rod would again command him. Gramps stepped back for a critical study.

"It'll do," he pronounced finally. "I pondered on starting you out with one of the old seven-ounce rods but what the dickens. You're going to fish for trout, you ought to begin right and you can't begin right 'thout the right tackle. Four and a half ounces this rod weighs 'thout the reel, and you'll be put to it to find a better. It took me a solid six weeks, working every night, to put her together the way I wanted her."

"Do you make these, too?"

"Yup. Something to do on long winter evenings."

"Breakfast," Gram announced. "They're only good while they're hot."

Bud laid his rod across two chairs and sat down to golden-brown griddle cakes, bacon and milk. He couldn't help looking at Gramps. At the other meals they had eaten together, Gramps' table manners had been correct enough. Now he didn't even seem to be thinking about food, as he put two pancakes together, laid two strips of bacon on the topmost pancake and doused everything with syrup. Then he rolled the bacon in the pancakes and ate the rolled mixture with his fingers. It was plain that in his thoughts he was already out on Skunk Creek. Gramps was no blasé sophisticate who had tasted all he could stomach of life by the time he was thirty. His eye to the grassroots, Gramps had long ago understood that everything was as old as creation itself and yet was eternally new. Nothing ever lost its sheen; some eyes just couldn't see it.

Gramps finished and looked meaningfully at Bud's place. Bud hastened to finish as Gramps rose.

"It isn't polite to eat and run, Mother, but the day's getting no younger. Ready, Bud?"

"All ready," Bud said, forebearing this time to add "Gramps."

"Bring me back at least one to eat, Delbert," Gram said. "I haven't had trout in almost three weeks."

"How'd you like Old Shark?" Gramps asked.

"I wouldn't," Gram sniffed. "In the first place, I'll

believe you have him when I see him. In the second, if you should get him, who's going to eat him after you're through showing him to everybody in Dishnoe County? I want an eating fish, not a showing trout."

"Sure," Gramps said.

Gramps brought another rod that was not jointed but had a reel on the reel seat. He gave Bud a leather-bound case similar to the one from which he'd taken dry flies last night, a limp leather case containing wet flies, and two leader boxes.

"Your flies and leaders," he explained. "If you're going to be a trout fisherman, you need your own tackle. Get your rod and come on."

Gingerly, hoping Gramps would carry it for him but taking it up himself when Gramps told him to, Bud tried to place his hand exactly as it had been when Gramps showed him how to balance a fine fly rod. After a little experimentation he found the proper grip, but his hand remained stiff on the butt. After looking appealingly at Gramps, who saw the look but pretended not to, Bud clenched his teeth and grimly resolved to carry through. Gramps went out first and Bud wondered how he would open the door after Gramps had closed it but Gramps stopped and held it open.

" 'Bye, Mother."

"Have a good time," Gram called. "Good-by, Allan."

"Good-by, ma'am."

To Bud's relief Gramps continued to hold the door open as if he had something else to say to Gram. Thus the first major hurdle was taken; Bud was out of the kitchen without either breaking his rod or anything else. Then, apparently forgetting what he intended to say, Gramps let the door close.

Shep rose to join them when they emerged onto the porch, but Gramps ordered him back. Ears drooping and looking abused, Shep sat down in front of the door and watched. When they were fifty yards away, he barked hopefully.

"It'll do you no good," Gramps said firmly. "Can't have a dog along when you're trout fishing," he said to Bud.

"Why?"

"He scares the trout."

"How can a dog scare trout?"

" 'Cause trout are scary, Bud. A shadow'll send 'em scooting and a dog can cast a shadow."

When they started down the path Bud had followed the night before, Bud's interest mounted. The black fawn lived there. Maybe he would see it again today. But as they walked along, resentment welled up in him, too. Gramps' rod was disjointed, which made it easy to carry. Bud's, however, had been left jointed so that he had constantly to be alert for every branch, every bush, and even every twig on every branch and bush. Bud thrust the tip of his rod into a hemlock tree and the rod bent alarmingly. Gramps, striding ahead, did not even bother to look around. Disgruntled, Bud disengaged his rod and hurried to catch up. He would have liked to carry a disjointed rod, too, but he didn't know how to take his apart and he wouldn't ask Gramps to show him.

Ten minutes later he was glad that Gramps was so eager to fish for Old Shark that he thought of nothing else. He was finding his rod easier to handle and he stopped gripping it desperately. He was becoming accustomed to its feel and balance, and beginning to understand it. And he hadn't called for help.

As they neared the thicket where the black fawn lived, Bud grew excited. But just before they came to it, Gramps swerved from the path into the woods. Bud kept his thoughts to himself. As much as he wanted to see the black fawn again, he wasn't going to ask Gramps to go out of the way for him.

The trees among which they threaded their way were mostly second-growth yellow birch but now and then there was a grove of aspens, a solitary black cherry or a copse of laurel and rhododendrons. It was such hard work to keep from tangling his rod in the twigs and branches that Bud almost bumped into Gramps before he was aware that the old man had stopped.

Gramps stood absolutely motionless and, without speaking, pointed. About a hundred yards away, a very dark-colored doe was leaping toward a copse of sheltering rhododendron. Behind her, matching his mother's every leap, ran the little black buck.

Now, Bud knew the fawn had not been abandoned. Just as Gramps had promised, his mother had come back to look for him and he was in safe care. And between last night and this morning, he had learned to use his legs. Not again, or at least not easily, would any human lay hands on him. The doe and fawn disappeared, and Gramps turned to Bud.

"There's your pal. After seeing his mammy, I know where he gets his color."

"Yes." Bud's eyes danced.

"I figured she'd take him away from that tote road after you and Shep found out where he was."

"Tote road?"

46

"The path we followed used to be a road. The lumbermen who cut the pine and hemlock that was in here made it and a hundred more like it."

"Why do they call them tote roads?"

Gramps shrugged. "I reckon 'cause they toted things back and forth on them."

"Were you here when the lumbermen came?"

"Saw the tail end of it but took no part. I wasn't much bigger'n that little black fawn. Been here ever since."

"When they cut the forests . . ." Bud began.

"We'd best get moving," Gramps said.

Gramps swerved at right angles to the direction they had been following and Bud wondered. Had Gramps brought him this way so Bud could see for himself that the black fawn was safe? If he had, what lay behind it? Bud was forced to concede that, if Gramps had deliberately set out to find the doe and fawn, he had shown wonderful woodcraft. Never once had he faltered or been at a loss as to the route to follow. He had known exactly where to find the doe and her baby.

Ten minutes later they reached Skunk Creek, a beautiful little woodland stream with pools of various sizes and depths and with sparkling riffles. Except for the larger pools, some of which were forty feet wide, the stream was less than a dozen feet wide. Most of Skunk Creek was bordered with willows and other trees, but the pool to which Gramps led Bud had almost no growth on the near bank and only scraggly willows on the far bank. Gramps laid his tackle on a moss-grown rock and turned to Bud.

"This ain't where Old Shark lives, but it's a darn' good place to show you how to lay a fly on the water. Let's have your rod."

Bud surrendered his rod. With skill honed to a razor's edge by vast experience, Gramps strung line through the guides, whipped the rod back and forth and paid out line from the reel as he did so. As he was keeping the line in the air, he said,

"See that little hunk of grass, maybe thirty-five feet out and a little up? I'll aim for it."

The rod described a graceful backward arc and an equally perfect forward sweep. The line glided forth as though it was not a flexible object at all, but a solid thing that Gramps was somehow shooting from the tip of his finger. The extreme tip of the line settled perfectly over the bit of grass. Gramps twitched it free, retrieved his line, and turned to Bud.

"Got it?"

Bud was flabbergasted.

"Try it and find out," Gramps said.

Bud took the rod, now strung and with a bit of line the length of the eight and a half foot rod dangling from the tip. But where the rod was a live thing in Gramps' hands, in Bud's it unaccountably went dead. He whipped it back, then forward, and the dangling line splashed at the very edge of the pool.

"You forgot to pay out line," Gramps said patiently. "You didn't use your reel. Let me show you."

He took the rod a second time, and once again laid the line smoothly on the water. Although Gramps had named no target, Bud knew that he was laying the line on the water exactly where he wanted it. Gramps returned the rod and Bud tried again. He remembered to pay out line as he cast, but the line slapped the water only about a dozen feet from shore and a full eight feet downstream from the target Bud had selected.

"You're throwing it," Gramps said, "and you're throwing with your whole arm. Here." He pressed the upper part of Bud's right arm against his ribs. "That's as much as you need and use your wrist. Let the rod work for you; don't you do everything."

Forty minutes later, although he couldn't come close to Gramps' distance or, unless the wildest luck was on his side, lay the line within two feet of any target he picked, Bud felt that he was improving. At least he was able to lay the line on the surface instead of whipping it into the water. Gramps tied a nine-foot tapered leader, a spiderweb at the thick end and like gossamer at the thin end, to Bud's line and showed him how to attach a dry fly to it. Then Gramps put a drop of oil on the fly, greased ten feet of line, and took the rod.

"Watch."

The fly soared out, hovered over the pool, settled on it precisely as a live insect might have, and began to float downstream. Gramps pulled the fly away from a small trout that rose and handed the rod to Bud.

"Go ahead."

Bud's first cast snagged a ground-hugging bush twenty feet behind him. The next time the fly bellied back to float beside the floating line. Then he hooked the only willow growing on the near side of the pool. But all the same Bud was elated. He forgot that the object of this wonderful art was to catch fish and, trying to remember all Gramps had told him, he kept on casting and learning through trial and error. When, after another hour, he was able to make ten successive casts and lay his fly reasonably well, Gramps pronounced judgment,

"Guess we can try now."

Without another word he turned and led the way downstream. Bud followed, knowing that his casting had not won the old man's approval but that Gramps had not wholly disapproved either. Bud did not care or at least he tried not to think about it, for he had discovered another new world. In time, he promised himself grimly, he would be a dry fisherman equal—well, almost equal—to Gramps.

Ten minutes later, Gramps slowed to a turtle's pace. He stole stealthily toward a twenty-foot-wide rock ledge that overhung a deep pool. When he came to the near border of the ledge, he turned and whispered,

"Leave your tackle. We'll crawl the rest of the way."

Bud laid his rod down carefully and, dropping to all fours, crawled beside Gramps toward the water. Five feet from the edge, Gramps dropped to his belly and began to inch toward the pool.

"No fast moves and show no more of yourself than you have to," Gramps whispered.

Bud nodded and wriggled toward the water. He peered down from the ledge and saw a broad, long pool formed by the ledge and fed by rushing riffles that curled around the upstream end of the ledge. On the far side the water was relatively shallow, or perhaps it only looked shallow because there was white sand on the bottom there. Schools of shiners and minnows swam lazily in that part of the pool and the white sand was pock-marked with driftwood that had floated down in flood time and, having become waterlogged, gone to the bottom.

At first glance the water at the near edge of the white sand seemed almost black. This was partly because the white sand ended and partly because the water was deeper there. Actually, it was green-blue, and the high-riding sun bored well into it.

Presently Bud saw a school of fish almost directly beneath him. The fish ranged in length from about five to nearly eighteen inches, and they lay very still in what appeared to be a quiet pocket of water, the biggest fish at the head of the school and the smallest at the end. Farther out, Bud saw more fish. The deepest part of the pool was too deep for the sun to penetrate it, and its invisible depths were tantalizing. Toward the foot of the pool, just before it was gathered in by the riffles that drained it, the trunk of a leaning sycamore jutted out about six feet over the water. The water near the sycamore was sun-sprayed, too. Bud saw flat stones on the bottom away from the bank, but in closer the bottom was in shadow and he could see nothing.

"The fish 'neath us are trout," Gramps whispered.

"Those farther out are suckers and mullets. The shallows 'cross the pool are loaded with minnows and shiners. Down there Old Shark hangs out 'neath that sycamore trunk." He spoke as reverently as a fanatic Moslem referring to Mecca.

"Stay here and watch. Don't move. You do, you'll send every trout in the pool kiting under the ledge."

Gramps wriggled backward and disappeared. A few minutes later Bud saw him near the foot of the ledge standing behind a rock spire that hid him from the pool and at the same time gave him freedom of action. Gramps made a perfect cast. The fly floated lazily toward the leaning sycamore and gathered speed as the water became swifter.

Old Shark rose and Bud saw him, a great, dark shadow that left the shaded bank and rose into the clear water upstream from the leaning sycamore. Old Shark did seem more like a shark than a trout as he paused within an inch of the fly and then sank back into the shadows from which he had come.

Almost unable to tear his eyes from Old Shark's lair, Bud's attention was distracted for a moment by a ripple in the water beneath him. It was a grasshopper struggling toward the ledge; before it reached safety, a twelve-inch trout from the school rose and took it.

Twenty minutes later Gramps called,

"Your turn. Take it slow and crawl away, mind you."

Bud took his place behind the spire of rock and cast. He knew how clumsy he was in comparison with Gramps, but he didn't care, for now he knew why Gramps spoke so reverently of Old Yellowfoot and Old Shark.

When Bud's second turn was over, he went back to where Gramps was sitting well back on the ledge.

"We didn't get him," Gramps said, but if he was disappointed he did not show it. "There's always another day and we'll come again. Reckon we'd better go in after this last try, though. Mother's all alone."

Bud stayed where he was and watched Gramps walk down to cast. A grasshopper the old man's feet had disturbed came to rest on Bud's left arm. He clapped his right hand over it and held the grasshopper until Gramps shrugged, reeled in and indicated that he was finished by hooking his fly in the cork butt of his rod.

Then, taking up his own rod, Bud strung the grasshopper on over the fly and crept across the ledge. He eased his grasshopper onto the water near the school of trout and a trout, which might well have been the one that had taken the other grasshopper, darted upward and sucked in the grasshopper. Bud struck, and

54

his rod bent and his line grew taut as the hooked trout tried frantically to escape.

"Keep the tip up! The tip up, Bud!" Gramps shouted.

With a heave that bent his rod double, Bud jerked the trout from the water and sent him ten feet back on the ledge, where he lay flapping. Bud raced back to get his catch.

"You did it!" Gramps shouted deliriously. "You did it! Your first trout on a dry fly!"

"I caught him on a grasshopper," Bud panted.

"What'd you say?" Gramps asked blankly.

"I caught him on a grasshopper."

"A hopper?"

"Yes."

"Surely you're not going to keep him?"

Bud looked at the ground without replying.

"Well," Gramps said with an effort, "I guess that's your business."

Without another word the old man turned to start homeward. Bud followed, miserable in the knowledge that he had betrayed Gramps. But even though it was abominable to take a trout on anything except a dry fly, he couldn't have done otherwise. Gram had asked them to bring her one trout.

THEY TOOK OLD SHARK ON THEIR SEVENTH TRIP TO the ledge. Gramps did it with a cunningly placed midge. Bud knew he would never forget the battle that followed or the plucking of Old Shark from shallow water when Gramps had finally worked him there.

They bore their prize proudly home, showed it to Gram. Then, in Gramps' asthmatic pickup truck—a vehicle that, until now, Bud had not even suspected was on the farm—they carried the trout to Pat Haley's store at Haleyville. Old Shark was a sensation and Pat Haley began at once to freeze him in a block of ice.

"What now?" Bud asked, as he and Gramps started home.

"Find us another big trout."

"I mean, what about Old Shark?"

"Oh, him. Even if he had any flavor and wasn't tougher'n a shoehorn, he's too much for us to eat. Nobody else'll want him for the same reasons." Gramps drove in silence for a while and then said, "Tell you what we'll do. When Pat's finished and everybody who wants a look at Old Shark has had it, we'll send him down to the orphanage. They don't often have trout there."

chapter 4

As he walked toward the road with a lunch pail dangling from one hand, it seemed to Bud that the driveway—endlessly long when he had labored up it that first day, with a chip on his shoulder and fear in his heart—had shrunken miraculously. He glanced quickly behind him to see if he was being watched and, seeing nobody, bent down to loosen the laces of the shiny black school shoes Gram had bought him in Haleyville. Then he straightened up and walked on, trying to manage a natural gait. But it was hopeless because after the conquest of Old Shark he had stopped wearing shoes. The soles of his feet had become so calloused that he could even run over the sharp stones around Gramps' gravel pit. Now, at the end of the summer, it had been so long since he had worn shoes that he felt as if he were dragging a ball and chain on each foot. His shoes pinched, too, but you could not go to school barefooted, not if Gram Bennett had anything to say about it.

The summer had been so wonderful that, looking back now that it was ending, every minute seemed precious. It had taken Bud a month to realize that there was actually only a bare minimum of work to be done and that Gram and Gramps had planned it that way. They had labored prodigiously to rear and educate seven sons and four daughters and, now that the children were grown up and had their own families, the old people had made up their minds to do the things they had always wanted to do. For Gramps that meant hunting and fishing; Gram wanted nothing more than to make other people happy. There was money in the bank and very little labor was needed to provide for the two old people even now that they had taken a hungry orphan into their home.

Bud reached the blacktop road and waited for the

bus to take him to the Haleyville Consolidated School, where he was to enter the eighth grade. He had concealed it from Gram and Gramps, but he dreaded starting out in a new school. As he stood there waiting, he tried to ease his troubled mind by concentrating instead on one of the high points of the summer.

He had cast a dry fly beneath a hollow stump beside a pool thickly bordered by a jungle of willows. The fly had gone truly and he had taken a fourteen-inch brook trout. Gramps had not been effusive, but it had meant a great deal to hear him say,

"Some day you'll be a fisherman, Bud."

Bud knew that although he might have learned to cast a dry fly, a single season or a dozen seasons do not necessarily produce a dry fly fisherman. There were very few masters of the art. Still, Gramps' approval was the next thing to achieving knighthood.

Sometimes with Gramps and sometimes alone, Bud had gone to see how the black fawn was faring. Although the fawn and doe had widened their range somewhat, they were still in the same general area. Now they were much more difficult to approach, but Bud had seen them enough times to know that the fawn was doing well. The knowledge that the fawn was flourishing made Bud less uneasy about his own good fortune, for since that first meeting, he had never stopped believing that a bond existed between himself and the fawn. Bud's luck had taken its turn for the better as soon as he found the little black buck and he was sure that misfortune would overtake him again if harm ever befell the fawn.

Bud had discovered the ruffed grouse, known locally as "pat'tidges," the thickets where foxes hunted and the places where black-masked raccoons washed their food. He had come to understand what sportsmanship means as opposed to hunting, and instead of recoiling when Gramps asked him to go grouse hunting, he had accepted eagerly and was looking forward to the opening day of the season.

Finally, he had found a dream of his own.

Gramps had a half-dozen turkeys, as many geese, a few ducks and a large flock of mongrel chickens that ranged from fussy little bantams to huge dunghill roosters. The flock was allowed to wander at will and to interbreed freely. According to the articles in the farm journals Bud had found stacked in the little closet off the living room, that was not the proper way to raise chickens. Although purebred fowls cost much more in the beginning, the returns were said to repay the initial investment many times over if the flock was correctly fed and housed. So far Bud had not broached the subject with Gram or Gramps because it was useless to talk about a project until you had the means to carry it out. Nevertheless, he had privately decided that, if and when he got both the money and Gram and Gramps' permission, he would buy a pen of pure-bred chickens and try to build up a flock.

That was for the future, but this was now, and when he saw the school bus approaching, Bud drew a deep breath. Then he clenched his teeth and boarded it.

The trip to Haleyville was over before he thought it could be, and the children assembled in little groups in front of the school. Bud went up alone to the entrance to the building and stood by himself with his back against the wall pretending to lounge nonchalantly. He was the only one who did not seem to know exactly where to go or what to do. Bells rang at intervals and the crowd of boys and girls thinned until the only ones left were Bud and a tall man who was obviously a teacher.

When Bud told him he was in the eighth grade, the teacher led Bud down several long corridors and past rows of closed doors with frosted glass panes in them. Finally he paused before one of the doors and, opening it, propelled Bud through ahead of him. A man with the physique of a wrestler but with gentle eyes looked around.

"I have one of your lost sheep, Mr. Harris," Bud's escort said.

"Come in and join the class, sheep," Mr. Harris said, smiling.

The class tittered and Bud writhed. The only refuge he knew was defiance.

"Don't call me names!" he shouted. "I'm not a sheep!"

"You're not very polite, either," Mr. Harris said without raising his voice. "What is your name?"

"Bud."

"Is that all your name? Just Bud?"

The class tittered again and Bud's mortification mounted as he choked out,

"Bud Sloan."

Mr. Harris consulted his class roll. "It says here you're Allan Sloan."

"I don't care what it says!" Bud shouted again. "My name's Bud!"

All at once he found himself sitting on the floor. Lights danced in his head. He blinked owlishly, and as if from a great distance, he heard Mr. Harris say,

"Get up, Allan. Your seat is the third one in the first row. Take it."

Bud walked to his seat and the class was subdued. Bud sat in sullen silence for the rest of the morning. When noon came, he ate a lonely lunch and when the dismissal gong sounded at the end of the day he was the first to rise.

"You're to stay after school, Allan," Mr. Harris said.

Scowling, Bud sat down again and watched his classmates whoop out to freedom. As though he had forgotten all about Bud or perhaps because Bud was too insignificant to notice, Mr. Harris methodically and calmly put his desk in order. Finally he looked up and said,

"Come on."

Mr. Harris led the way out through the rear entrance and Bud gulped as they neared the parking lot. He would have run if his legs would have obeyed him, but since they would not, he got into Mr. Harris's car. They started up the road toward the Bennetts' farm, and after they were out of town, Mr. Harris said,

"You needed that cuffing I gave you."

Bud said nothing as Mr. Harris continued, "You had it coming and you know it. I know exactly what you were thinking and why. Stop thinking it.

"Let me tell you about another boy," Mr. Harris said, "another orphan. He was farmed out when he was just about your age, and he went to a new school exactly as you did. Inside, he was frightened as a rabbit with five dogs and nine cats backing him into a corner, but he was afraid to let anyone else know that. The teacher reprimanded him and he shouted at him. Then, because he was convinced that only tough guys can get along, he hit the teacher with a chair. The boy was twelve when it happened. He was eighteen when he finally got out of reform school, and it was a reform school even if they called it a training school for boys."

Bud said nothing and Mr. Harris went on, "It's a true story, as I should know. The boy's name was Jeffrey Chandler Harris, who now teaches eighth grade at Haleyville Consolidated School. I've wished many a time that that teacher had had sense enough to clobber me when I most needed it."

Before Bud could recover or reply, Mr. Harris eased his car to a stop in front of the drive leading to Gram and Gramps' house and was holding out his hand.

"Friends?"

"Friends," Bud said, and shook hands.

64

THE AUTUMN DAYS WERE LITERALLY GOLDEN DAYS. Gold leaves clung to the aspens and birches and to some of the maples. Goldenrod bloomed. A golden moon shone down on a field where golden pumpkins lay among shocked corn. The sun rose golden every morning and set in a golden blaze every night.

Most of the crops were harvested and the fields lay bare. The cellar beneath the farmhouse was bursting with the fruits and vegetables that could be stored, and every shelf was filled with jars in which Gram had canned those that could not be stored. Split and neatly corded wood was stacked up to the roof of the woodshed and now the wood boxes on the back porch and in the kitchen were kept heaping full.

The warmth the kitchen range radiated was welcome these days, for even at high noon there was a sharp tang in the air. The cattle preferred the sunny to the shady parts of the pasture and a box, which had a hole cut in it and with a cloth hung over the hole, covered Shep's bed on the porch.

After their first encounter Bud and Mr. Harris had understood each other and Bud brought home a very creditable first report card. That afternoon he raced up to his room to exchange school clothes for work clothes and ran back down the stairs, stopping in the kitchen only long enough to gobble the cookies and drink the milk Gram had ready for him.

"I have to hurry and help Gramps get everything caught up so we can go grouse hunting," he explained when Gram remonstrated.

"Oh. That's real important. Scoot, now."

Bud drank the last of his milk and ran out. In the corn field Gramps had the team hitched to the light box wagon and was walking beside it and lifting ripe pumpkins into the box, starting and stopping the horses with his voice alone. Bud raced toward Gramps, and Shep came leaping to meet him. As he petted the big furry dog, Bud looked toward the autumn woods and for an instant he thought he had caught a glimpse of the black fawn melting away into the trees.

For Bud the fawn was outside the laws of nature, but with the taking of Old Shark he had learned the difference between sport for sport's sake and killing for killing's sake. Actually, as Gramps had explained, it was not only fair, it was wise to harvest some creatures. Old Shark, for instance, had been a ravenous old tyrant who had consumed vast amounts of food, including smaller trout; now that he was gone, the trout left in the pool would have a better chance. Gramps had made Bud see that it was, in fact, kind to harvest the surplus game crop because there is enough food for only a limited number of wild creatures. The rest must die, and the ways of nature are almost always crueler and more prolonged than death at the hand of a hunter.

Bud thought that the swift-winged grouse were among the most fascinating of wild creatures. He almost never saw them until they thundered into flight, a thing that never failed to startle him. They were birds of mystery to him and he could not help being excited because he and Gramps were going to hunt grouse when the season opened. Safe in its case in Bud's room was a trim little double-barreled twenty-gauge shotgun, and as soon as the last of the crops was in, Gramps had promised to show him how to use it.

Shep bounced ahead to frolic around Gramps, and Gramps stopped work as Bud came up to him.

"Hi, Bud."

"Hello, Gramps. I hurried so I can help load the rest of the pumpkins."

"Well now, that's right decent of you. But you won't be sorry. A man ain't lived 'til he's helped load and haul punkins. Did you ever stop to consider what a remarkable thing a punkin is? You can look at 'em and tell what the weather's been by the looks of the punkin, so they're a weather table. You can just about tell the season by the looks of a punkin, so that makes 'em a calendar. You can bounce one off somebody's head and knock him sillier'n the cow that jumped over the moon and still not hurt him, so they're a weapon. You can turn 'em into goblins on Halloween, and you can eat 'em. Yep. A punkin's a right remarkable outfit."

"How are they most remarkable?" Bud asked.

"In punkin pie. Let's get to work."

When they had loaded the wagon, Gramps unwrapped the reins that had been around the wagon's center post, drove to where the great, outer cellar doors yawned wide, and two by two they carried the pumpkins into the cellar. Then, while Bud stabled and cared for the horses, and pitched hay down the chute for the cows, Gramps milked.

That night, after the evening meal, Bud gave himself to the complexities of English, arithmetic and American history while Gram knitted and Gramps pored over the latest issue of *The Upland Gunner*. Bud's eyes stole from his textbook to the magazine in Gramps' hands, and although he made a prodigious effort to return to the conjugation of irregular verbs, he found it a hopeless task. He raised his eyes again to the magazine, which had a gorgeous front cover showing a woodcock in flight, two English setters on perfect point and a hunter who was obviously about to add the woodcock to his bag.

Gramps spoke from behind the magazine, "That was a mighty fine report card you fetched home, Bud."

"Thanks, Gramps."

"You fetch home reports like that, and you'n me will have a whack at Old Yellowfoot sure after we're done with the grouse."

Without bothering to find out how Gramps had managed to peer through the magazine and discover that he was not studying, Bud returned to his textbook. Gramps had given him the incentive he needed at the moment, but on a farm everybody has his tasks and Bud knew without being told that his chief one was to get everything he could from his school work.

When Bud came home from school the next day, Gramps was sitting on the back porch with the twenty-gauge shotgun, Bud's gun, across his knees. Nearby was a wooden cleaning rod, some strips of white cloth, a can of nitro solvent and a can of oil. As though such an occupation was too commonplace to call for any explanation, Gramps said,

"Best get moving."

"Moving?"

"Now doggone! You didn't think I'd take you grouse hunting 'thout you know which end of the gun the shot comes out of, did you?"

Bud changed his clothes in frantic haste, gulped down the milk Gram had waiting and caught up some cookies. Gramps looked at him reprovingly as he burst out the back door.

"You ain't going to a fire. Slow and easy's the way you take her when you're hunting. Come on."

He led the way to a windmill behind the barn. Before the farmers along the road had organized to form their own water company, the windmill had pumped all the Bennetts' water. The wind furnished power when it blew. When it did not, a gasoline engine operated the pump. Even though there was another supply of water now, Gramps had not let the windmill deteriorate in case it should be needed again.

While Bud had been at school, Gramps had hung cans by eight-foot cords from each of the vanes of the windmill and hooked up power belts so the engine would turn the windmill. A hundred feet away he had also put up two wooden standards that looked like sign posts and covered them with newspapers.

Two boxes of shotgun shells were laid out on the engine mount. Gramps picked up one.

"Some people practice shoot on live pigeons," he said. "I don't hold with that 'cause I don't hold with killing anything for no good reason. Some shoot at tin cans tossed in the air, but that's no way to learn 'cause tossed cans just ain't fast enough. Some shoot clay pigeons, which is all right if you got the money. I have my own way. Now you know about choke?"

"Yes, Gramps."

"Tell me."

"The left barrel of this gun is full choke, which means that it has a narrower opening than the right and will shoot a closer pattern, but it also has a longer range. It's to be used for birds flying a considerable distance away."

Gramps nodded and took two shells from the box. "Load her."

Bud flipped the lever that broke the barrels and slipped a shell into each. He tried to do it very calmly, but in spite of himself his hands shook. He had broken the barrels a hundred times before and in imagination he had loaded the gun and sighted on a speeding bird a thousand times. But this was the first time he had ever held the gun armed with live ammunition. He did not forget to check the safety, and Gramps noticed but said nothing.

The old man said, "So you can see for yourself what pattern means, and the difference between a full and modified choke, shoot your left barrel into the left paper and the right into the right."

Bud braced the gun stock against his shoulder, sighted on the right-hand paper, braced himself, and pulled the trigger. The gun's blasting roar was much louder than anything he had expected, but the recoil was almost negligible. He shot the left barrel with more confidence.

"You flinched on the first but held steady on the second," Gramps pronounced. "Now let's see what happened."

They walked forward and Bud studied both papers. The one to the left shot with a full choke bore a roughly circular pattern of evenly distributed pellets that had gone through the paper and imbedded themselves in the wood backing. The target shot with the modified barrel was pock-marked with such a wide circle that it was obvious not all of them could have struck the paper.

"Understand?" Gramps queried.

"I understand."

"Then we'll get on, and since anybody who'd shoot a bird on the ground would catch a trout on a grasshopper, like a certain party did on Skunk Crick, we shoot 'em on the wing. Just a minute."

Gramps started the gasoline engine. The windmill vanes began to whirl and the dangling cans, gaining momentum, strained at the ends of their strings. Taking the shotgun, Gramps fired one barrel, then the other, and two of the whirling cans leaped wildly. He gave the shotgun and a pair of shells to Bud.

Bud shot, but although he knew he was on target, he missed the can at which he had aimed. He shot again and again until he had scored twenty-three consecutive misses. Then, all at once, he found the feel and balance of his gun. It was no longer a separate thing but a part of himself. With Gramps' coaching him on leading, or shooting ahead of the target, he scored two hits, missed three and scored ten straight.

"You're real good at shooting tin cans on the wing," Gramps pronounced. "Now we'll see how good you are on grouse. Saturday's the day, Bud."

chapter 5

THE FRIDAY AFTER THE target practice the sky was overcast when Bud came home from school and the wind was variable. There was a wintry tang in the air. The day that Bud had thought would never come was tomorrow.

Less than half aware of what he was doing, or of how he was doing it, Bud helped with the nightly chores and made no serious mistakes simply because by now he could do them by rote. He returned to earth long enough to enjoy Gram's excellent supper and afterward tried to concentrate on his school books, which might as well have been written in Sanskrit. Finally he gave himself up to dreaming.

Shotgun in hand, he was walking slowly through crisp autumn woods. A grouse, a wary old cock bird that had been taught by experience how to avoid hunters, rose in front of him. The grouse flew into a rhododendron thicket and, keeping brush between Bud and himself, was seen only as a hurtling ball of feathers and at uncertain intervals. Bud, the master sportsman, made a swift mental calculation of the bird's line of flight, aimed where he knew it would reappear and scored a hit so perfect that even Gramps was impressed. With complete nonchalance befitting a hunter, Bud retrieved his trophy and said casually, "Not a bad grouse."

"And not a bad hunter!" Gramps ejaculated. "I've been practicing on these babies for more than forty years, and I never saw a finer shot!"

"Hadn't you better go to bed, Allan?" Gram asked, bringing him back to reality.

"You said," Gramps chuckled, "that you've been practicing on these babies for more than forty years and never saw a finer shot. What were you shooting at, Bud?"

Bud wriggled in embarrassment, knowing that he

had once again invited disaster by revealing his thoughts. But it was no longer the risk that it would have been a few short months ago, for neither Gram nor Gramps had shown any sign of wanting to exploit his weaknesses. He grinned and said sheepishly,

"I must have been thinking out loud."

"You're tired," Gram said soothingly. "Now you just run along."

He said good night and for a moment before crawling into bed stood at the window. Then he caressed the cased shotgun, got into bed and pulled the covers up. Five minutes later wind-driven snow began to rattle crisply against his bedroom window.

It was a magic sound that seemed to bring Bennett's Woods and all they contained into Bud's bedroom. He imagined he saw the black buck, a well-grown fawn now, pawing snow aside to get at the vegetation beneath, while his mother flirted coyly nearby with Old Yellowfoot. Cottontail rabbits played on the snow and sharp-nosed foxes sought them out. Blue jays huddled on their roosts and dreamed up new insults to scream at the world. Tiny chickadees, tiny puffs of feathers never daunted by even the bitterest winter weather, chirped optimistically to one another in the night.

Bud's imagination always returned to the grouse that left their three-toed tracks, like small chicken tracks, clearly imprinted in the new snow as they sought out the evergreen thickets where they would be sure of finding food and shelter from the first biting blast of winter. Bud followed the tracks. The grouse burst out of their thickets like feathered bombs and each time he choose his bird and never missed.

It occurred to him suddenly that, even though no hint of daylight showed against his window, he must have overslept. Bud sprang hastily up and consulted the battered clock on his dresser to find he had been in bed for only an hour. And so he returned to more dreams of grouse.

Always he found them by first locating their tracks and following them into the thicket. Grouse after grouse fell to his deadly aim while Gramps, who couldn't even hope to match this kind of shooting, finally stopped trying and stood by admiringly. Then without any warning, Bud was confronted by a gigantic cock grouse whose head towered a full two feet over his own. Bud halted in his tracks, first astonished and then afraid. When he turned to run, the grouse ran after him, snapped him up in its bill, and began to shake him as Shep shook the rats that he sometimes surprised around the barn. As the giant grouse shook him, it said in a thunderous voice that Bud had already shot nine hundred grouse, far more than any one hunter should ever take, and now he must face his just punishment.

Bud awoke in a cold sweat to find Gramps shaking his shoulder. "Time to move," Gramps said, and left.

Bud shook off the remnants of sleep as only a youngster can and remembering the snow that had rattled against his window during the night, rushed across the floor to look out. The barn roof was starkly white in the early morning gloom, and the earth was snow-covered. Bud ran to the chair beside his bed where he stacked his clothing and dressed hurriedly, aware of the cold for the first time. He pulled on and laced his rubber-bottomed pacs, and then took up his shotgun affectionately and ran down the stairs.

As anxious as he was to be in the woods, it never occurred to Bud that he was free to surrender to anxiety and be on with the hunting. It was right to anticipate but not to fret because first the stock had to be tended and fed. The farm creatures were utterly helpless and dependent, and the humans whose chattels they were had a responsibility to them. Bud came into the kitchen where Gram was busy and said cheerfully,

"Good morning, ma'am."

"Good morning, Allan."

As he was putting on a jacket so he could rush out and help Gramps with the morning chores, Bud stopped with his arm half in and half out of the sleeve. Gram's face was wan and her smile was tired, and sudden fear leaped in Bud's heart. Nothing could possibly go wrong with Gram, but obviously something had gone wrong. Bud said because he had to say something,

"I'm going out to help Gramps."

"Wait just a minute," Gram said as though she had just made up her mind, "I'd like to talk with you."

"Yes?" Bud said uncertainly.

"Will you watch over Gramps very carefully today, Allan?"

Bud was speechless, for Gramps was like one of the great white oaks that grew in Bennett's Woods, or one of the granite boulders that reared their humped backs on the hills. He watched over everything and everybody. With Gram, he made the Bennett farm a happy fortress where people could live as people were meant to live. Being asked to watch over Gramps made Bud feel small and incompetent.

"Is Gramps sick?" he asked.

"No," and he knew that she was speaking only half the truth. "It's just that he isn't as young as he used to be and I don't like to see him go in the woods alone."

"Perhaps we should stay home?"

"Oh no!" Gram said vehemently. "That would be far worse than going. Gramps was never meant for a rocking chair. Just watch over him."

Bud threw his arms around her. He was a little surprised, now that they stood so close together, to discover that he did not have to rise at all to kiss her seamed cheek. He had always thought of Gram as being far taller than he, but now he knew she wasn't at all.

"Don't you worry, Gram. I'll take care of him."

"Now I just knew you would!" There was a sudden, happy lilt in Gram's voice and her weariness had disappeared.

Bud kissed her again and went into the snowy morning, and if some of his zest had evaporated, something better had taken its place. He had known almost from the beginning how desperately he needed Gram and Gramps, and his greatest fear had been that, somehow, he would be separated from them. The thought of parting from them had worried him endlessly, and he had schemed to make himself indispensable. But there seemed to be no way, for he was not indispensable; he wasn't even important. Now, miraculously, the way had opened. Without understanding just how it had been brought about, Bud knew that Gram and Gramps needed him, too, and the knowledge gave him new stature and strength, and broke the final barriers that had held him aloof. It was impossible to remain distant when Gram's very heart cried out to him.

The brisk wind whirled little snow devils across the yard and the barn roof was covered with snow. Shep came out of the partly open door to meet him, and Bud stooped to ruffle his ears. The collie remained by his side as Bud entered the barn, which was warm from the heat given off by the animals' bodies.

As he was milking Cherub, the only cow of the four that would kick if she caught the milker off guard, Gramps looked up and said happily, "It's a great day for it."

"It looks that way, Gramps," said Bud, his apprehension lessening in the face of Gramps' enthusiasm. "I'll get to work."

He got his own pail and started milking Susie, thinking of the time when milking had seemed an art so involved that only a genius could master it. Now Bud could match Gramps' milking skill. He rose to empty his full milk pail into the can standing in the cooler. In another hour or so, Joe Travis would be along to collect it with his truck and carry it to the creamery at Haleyville. Household milk for both drinking and churning was always saved from the last pail. Gram still poured milk into shallow pans in the cool cellar, and separated milk from cream by skimming off the cream with a great spoon when it rose to the top of the pan.

Coming back to milk the last cow, Bud stood aside so Gramps could pass with his brimming pail and said,

"If you want to finish Clover, I'll take care of the horses and chickens."

"Hop to it," Gramps said cheerfully. "Though I'd like to get going there's no tearing rush. Those grouse are going to stay where it's warm."

Breathing a silent prayer because his ruse had worked —it was easier to milk another cow than to fork down hay for the horses and care for the poultry—Bud went to the horse stable. Tied to mangers, the two placid horses raised their heads and nickered a soft welcome when he entered. Bud filled the mangers with hay, gave each horse a heaping measure of grain, filled their water containers, groomed them and went on to the poultry house.

82

The turkeys, geese and ducks had long since gone to one of the freezing lockers Pat Haley kept in the rear of his store, where, dressed and plucked, they awaited the various winter holidays and the home-comings of the Bennetts' children and grandchildren. Most of the chickens remained alive, however. A few were still on the roosts, and in the dim light, none was very active.

As Bud filled the mash and grain hoppers and checked the supply of crushed oyster shell, he day-dreamed about the flock he hoped to have. Instead of these mongrel chickens, he visualized an evenly matched, evenly colored flock. This morning he fa-vored Rhode Island Reds, but sometimes he was for White Leghorns, or Anconas, or one of the many varieties of Plymouth Rocks or White or Buff Wyan-dottes. Bud had not yet decided whether it was better to breed for eggs or meat, or to choose a species of fowl that would supply both. But he did know that he wanted chickens. Although he never saw himself reaping great wealth from them, in his imagination he often heard himself assuring Gram and Gramps that the egg money, or the broiler money, depending on the breed he happened to fancy at the moment, was ample to pay all the current bills and leave a substantial reserve.

He finished and he had no sooner shut the hen-house door than he ceased being a poultryman and became a hunter. The light was stronger now, the new snow was soft beneath his pacs and the wind was cold enough so that the season's first snow would not melt. The snow gave a special glamour to the forth-coming hunt, for in all the hunting stories Bud had liked the hunters had worked on snow. Moreover, the snow and the cold wind would keep the grouse concen-trated in or near their evergreen thickets, and since Gramps knew every thicket in Bennett's Woods, the shooting would be fine.

Gramps was at the table paying no attention to what he ate or how he ate it. Gram started to fill Bud's plate as he came in, and she looked at him meaningfully: he was to watch over Gramps and Gram knew that he would. But all she said was,

"Get them while they're hot, Allan."

"Sure, Gram," Bud said cheerfully.

As he was about to stuff two pancakes rolled around two strips of bacon and doused with syrup into his mouth, Gramps stopped with the food halfway from his plate.

"What'd you call Mother?"

"Gram," Bud said, and now it seemed that he had never called her by any other name.

"Why of course, Delbert," Gram said. "Where have your ears been?"

"Wish I knew," Gramps said, and resumed eating.

They finished, pushed their plates back, and Bud donned a belt-length wool jacket over his wool shirt. He stuffed the pockets full of shotgun shells, caught up his shotgun and kissed Gram again.

" 'Bye. We'll bring you back something nice."

"Just bring yourselves back safely, and have a good time."

They left the house, and when Shep fell in beside them, Gramps did not order him back. Bud said nothing. He had learned long ago why Shep scared trout, for the smallest shadow that fell across their pool would send trout scurrying for the shelter of overhanging banks or into crannies beneath rocks. It stood to reason that Shep would also frighten grouse, but that was a different matter. When Bud and Gramps approached, the grouse were sure to be frightened anyway and a dog prowling about was as likely to offer shots by sending grouse rocketing skyward as he was to frighten them out of range.

Bud stole a sidewise glance at Gramps and saw nothing amiss. But he was troubled by Gramps' silence until the old man spoke,

"When'd it happen, Bud?"

"When did what happen?"

"You called Mother 'Gram.' You kissed her when we left."

"Well," Bud said, and then he came out with it, "I've wanted to do it for a long time."

"A body ought to do what he wants more often," Gramps said. "Maybe it'd make a heap of people feel a heap better a lot sooner. Do you like it here with us?"

"Oh, yes!"

"So'd our young'uns, but after they grew up, they couldn't wait to leave. That's right and as it should be; the old have no call to tell the young what they must do. What are you aiming to be when you grow up?"

"I haven't thought."

"Don't you want to do anything?"

"Yes. I want to raise chickens," Bud said recklessly.

"Raise chickens!" Gramps was surprised. "How come? Tell me."

Bud told him of the agricultural journals he had found in the closet off the living room and of the articles he had read about chickens, which had convinced him that the farm's present flock ought to be exchanged for purebreds. At any rate, he told Gramps, as soon as he could somehow earn enough money to buy a small pen of purebreds, he wanted to test his theory, if he could have Gram and Gramps' permission.

"Guess we can find room for a few more chickens. We'll think about it," Gramps said when Bud finished. Then he lowered his voice to a whisper. "We'd best take it easy. Should be grouse round this next bend."

Noting that Shep had left them for an excursion of his own, Bud balanced the shotgun with both hands and poised his thumb to slip the safety catch. They rounded the bend and stopped in their tracks.

About a hundred and fifty feet away there was a dense thicket of young hemlocks, small bushy trees about eight feet high. Ten feet from the thicket, so still that at first he seemed to be a statue rather than a living thing, stood a mighty buck. His head was turned toward them and his ears flicked forward as he tested the wind with his black nose. From the tip of his nose to the tip of his tail, every line was graceful and yet brutally powerful. His craggy antlers curved high and spread wide. As little as he knew about deer, Bud knew his antlers were superb. From the hocks and knees down, each of the buck's feet was a light yellow.

An instant later the buck had melted like a ghost into the hemlocks and Gramps said in awed tones,

"Old Yellowfoot!"

Bud looked again where the legendary buck of Bennett's Woods had been, half expecting to see him still there. But Old Yellowfoot was gone without a sound. It seemed impossible for so large an animal to have faded out of sight so quickly, and for a moment Bud wondered if he really had been there. But he had seen Old Yellowfoot, the buck no hunter ever saw fully.

"Was that really Old Yellowfoot?" he asked.

"That was him right enough!" Gramps said.

"We might have shot him."

"With a couple of shotguns and number six shot?" Gramps said. "Don't fool yourself, Bud. That old buck knows as well as we do that we wouldn't no more'n sting him if we did shoot, and he knew we wouldn't shoot 'cause he knows it ain't deer season."

"How does he know?"

Gramps said seriously, "I don't know how he knows it, but I'm sure he does. Naturally deer don't carry calendars, but they do tick off the days 'bout as accurately as we can and Old Yellowfoot's been through a lot of deer seasons. He can smell danger far's we can a skunk. If we'd been coming up here with a couple of thirty-thirtys, in deer season, we wouldn't have got within sniffing distance. I told you that buck's smarter'n most people. Wait'll we get on his tail and you'll see for yourself."

They came to the place where the big buck had been standing and examined the hoofprints that were clearly defined in the snow. They were bigger than any deer tracks Bud had ever seen, and there seemed to be something mystical about them just because they were Old Yellowfoot's.

Shep panted up, wagging his tail agreeably. He sniffed briefly at Old Yellowfoot's tracks and sat down in the snow. Gramps skirted the hemlocks, eyes to the ground, and presently he called,

"They're in here."

Advancing to Gramps' side, Bud saw that half a dozen grouse had gone from the open woods into the little evergreens. Bud looked into the grove trying to penetrate the closely interlaced branches. It seemed hopeless. If the copse could swallow Old Yellowfoot as though he had melted into the air, how could you expect to find the grouse?

"Let's go in," Gramps said.

They entered the copse, Gramps following the grouse tracks and Bud ten feet to one side. Bud's shotgun was half raised, ready to snap to shooting position at his shoulder, and his pulse was throbbing with excitement. Too eager, he pushed a few feet ahead of Gramps but fell back at once so that, when the grouse rose, both of them would have an equal chance to shoot. Bud knew that otherwise Gramps wouldn't dare shoot for fear of hitting him.

The grouse rose so suddenly and unexpectedly that for a moment Bud forgot his gun. He had thought they would be deeper in the thicket. Gramps' gun blasted, and Bud saw a grouse pitch from the air into the snow. Then they were gone.

"I didn't hear you shoot," Gramps said.

"I couldn't get ready."

There was the suspicion of a chuckle in his voice, but Gramps' face was perfectly solemn when he faced Bud. "There'll be more," he said.

As they went forward, the only grouse that had not yet risen rocketed up beneath their feet. Bud saw the bird clearly as it soared over the tops of the hemlocks. He raised his gun and after he had shot, a shower of hemlock twigs filtered earthward from a place two feet beneath and three feet to one side of where the bird had been. Bud shuffled his feet and looked bewildered. "You get too excited," Gramps said. "Take it easier." "Yes, Gramps," Bud said meekly.

They broke out of the other side of the thicket and came upon the place where Old Yellowfoot had left the hemlocks to slink into a stand of yellow birch. The tracks were not those of a running or excited deer, for Old Yellowfoot hadn't kept his regal antlers by surrendering to excitement. He had walked all the way and by this time was probably back in some hiding place that only he knew.

Now they were in a thicket of small pines which were more scattered than the hemlocks had been. Grouse tracks led into it, and Gramps tumbled another bird out of the air. Bud saw one running on the snow, and he slipped the safety and aimed. He almost shot, but at the last moment released his finger tension on the trigger and let the bird run out of sight. That was not the way to take grouse.

Two hours and fifteen shots later, they came to still another thicket and prepared to work through it. Gramps was no longer shooting, for even though the limit was four grouse, half the limit was enough for anyone. Bud's cheeks were burning, and he was grimly determined as they went on. Gramps had two grouse with two shots; he had none with fifteen. Then the grouse went up.

This time it was different. Just as when he had been shooting at the tin cans tied to the windmill, his gun became a part of him and he seemed to be directed by something outside of himself.

Bud swung on a grouse, shot and saw the bird fold its wings and tumble gracefully. Then he swung on a second bird and that one, too, dropped to the earth. He had shot fifteen times without coming even close to a grouse, but now he had redeemed himself by scoring a double. Not even Gramps had done that, and Bud turned proudly to the old man.

Gramps was on his knees, trying desperately to keep from going all the way down by bracing himself with his shotgun. His head was bent forward as though he was too tired to hold it up, and what Bud could see of his face was blue. Gramps' breath came in hoarse, far-apart gasps—the most terrifying sound the boy had ever heard.

chapter   6

ALTHOUGH HE FOR-
got the grouse he had just shot, Bud remembered to
lean his shotgun against a little pine. That was something he could not forget, for he had been too long
with too little not to know the worth of whatever
finally came his way, and the shotgun was precious.
Having put the gun where it was safe, he went to
Gramps.

Bud's heart constricted with fear as he strode forward, but he did not panic and it never even occurred
to him to wish somebody else was there to help. Not

once in his life had Bud been able to run or even shrink from a problem, and the pattern was set indelibly. He felt like sobbing because Gramps was in trouble, but he knew he had to do all he could to help. Wondering how Gram had known this might happen, Bud knelt beside him, passed his right arm around the old man's shoulders and took Gramps' shotgun in his left hand.

Gramps tried to speak, but he was unable to, and after relinquishing his shotgun to Bud, he sank back heavily to a sitting position. Bud tightened his right arm around Gramps' shoulder and slipped behind him to give additional support with his shoulder. He did not know what was the matter with Gramps, but he knew it was serious and that it would do Gramps no good to be allowed to fall backward in the snow. Bud had no idea what else to do except to get Gramps back to the house as soon as possible. For the present there was nothing to do but wait.

Gramps' head remained slumped forward and his breath continued to come in wheezes. He was as tense as a strung bow; even beneath Gramps' hunting jacket Bud could feel taut muscles. But Gramps did not move or even try to move.

It was unthinkable to leave him for even the short

time it would take to run to the farm and return with a sled. While Bud was trying to think of a way to drag the old man back to the house, Gramps' head snapped backward and jerked forward. He coughed violently and his head slumped forward again. All at once the rattling gasps stopped, leaving silence almost as terrifying as the agonized breathing had been. Then Gramps said faintly, but with unmistakable disgust,

"I ought to be old enough to know better! Blamed nonsense!"

He raised his head and Bud saw that his face was no longer blue. But in spite of the cold wind, a thin film of sweat glistened on the old man's face. As Bud wiped it off with his handkerchief, he could see that Gramps was not so tense and that the great vein in his neck, which had been throbbing furiously, had subsided.

"Did I scare you, Bud?" Gramps said, raising his head and smiling.

"Uh-huh."

"Shouldn't have," Gramps said. "Wasn't any good reason for it. Just a pile of blamed nonsense."

"Can you sit up without help?" Bud asked.

"What do you think I am? A baby? Sure I can sit up."

"I'll make a sled and have you back to the house in a jiffy."

"You'll make a sled?" Gramps said in something like his old voice. "Just how do you aim to make it?"

"I don't know," Bud said grimly, "but I'll make one."

"I believe you would," Gramps conceded. "I believe you would do just that, but it ain't necessary. I'll walk back."

And with a sudden lurch, Gramps heaved himself to his feet. He teetered uncertainly, but before Bud could help, Gramps found his balance and stood steadily. His face was pale, but he was no longer sweating and his grin was warm.

"See? Sound as a yearling colt. Now you stop troubling your head about me and find those two pat'tidges you dropped."

Then Bud remembered the pair of grouse that had fallen to his two shots. He looked at his shotgun, which was still leaning against the little pine very near his shooting position when he scored his double. He reconstructed the approximate positions of the two grouse when he shot, and the angle at which each had pitched into the snow. He looked uncertainly at Gramps.

"Go ahead," the old man said. "You put 'em down and now you get 'em. There's two things you don't leave in the woods; one's wounded game and t'other's dead game. You get 'em."

Bud caught up his shotgun, cradled it in the crook of his arm, and walked to where he thought the first bird would be. He found it almost at once, pitched against a little cluster of blackberry canes with its wings still spread as though it were ready to fly again. For the second bird Bud searched five minutes. He put both in the game pocket of his jacket and returned to Gramps.

"I found them."

"Good." Except that he was still pale, Gramps seemed almost his old self. "That was nice shooting, Bud."

Bud nodded, too worried even to smile. Any other time Gramps' admission that Bud had shot well would have been overwhelming, for although Gramps seldom condemned harshly, he almost never praised at all.

"I guess," Gramps said with forced cheer, "we might as well go tell Mother the hunt's over."

Bud said nothing. Gramps had recovered sufficiently so that he could risk running to the house for the toboggan that lay across two wooden horses in the barn.

But he did not offer to go, for he sensed something that did not appear on the surface. It was something that had taken root the day Gramps was born and grown stronger with every day of his life. Gramps had walked here; he would walk back, and Bud knew that to suggest Gramps could not walk out without help would wound him deeply. Even while he felt guilty because he did not ignore Gramps' wishes and go for the toboggan anyway, Bud still sympathized. He, too, thought that a man should stand on his own feet.

Trying not to appear obvious, Bud adjusted his gait to the old man's. It was far slower than usual, but Gramps seemed not to notice that everything was not as it should be, and Bud was grateful. Shep came out of the woods to join them. He trotted twenty feet ahead, looked back to make sure they were following, and then set a pace that kept him about twenty feet in the lead. They were halfway to the farm when Gramps spoke,

"There's no call to say anything to Mother 'bout this."

"She should know," Bud said.

"She should," Gramps agreed. "If it was anything bad she sure should. But it's just a heap of blamed nonsense. Doc Beardsley told me that himself. 'Most twenty-five years ago a horse kicked me in the head. It never fazed me then, but seems like it's showing up now, and Doc says I can expect these little cat fits every now'n again. They don't mean any more than a headache or sore tooth. You wouldn't want to worry Gram, would you?"

Bud said reluctantly, "No."

"She will worry if you tell her."

Bud looked down at the snow. Gram couldn't have known that Gramps would be stricken, but she had certainly known that he *might* be. Bud stole a look at Gramps, who had started to walk almost at his normal pace and who now bore only faint traces of his recent ordeal. If it was serious, Gram should know. But if, as Gramps said, it was only a trifling incident, it would only worry Gram to know. Bud reached his decision.

"I won't tell her," he promised.

"A right smart idea," Gramps said. "A fair half of the world's trouble is brought on by people shooting off their mouths when they'd do a lot better to keep 'em shut. You have plenty of horse sense, Bud."

Bud thought suddenly of the little black buck, and he felt an almost uncontrollable yearning to seek him out. The buck was his brother, through whom Bud had

99

discovered the first key that had helped open a series of magic doors. The black buck, Bud felt, would help him reach the correct decision now about whether Gram should know. But the buck was not at hand, and now they were too near the house not to continue.

Gramps asked, far too casually, "How do I look?"

Bud said, "All right," and Gramps did look all right —a bit tired, perhaps, and a little pale, but not like a man who had been as desperately ill as he had been. They brushed the snow from their pacs and entered the kitchen.

Gram looked intently at Gramps. "Do you feel all right, Delbert?"

Gramps said, "Nope. Anybody with half an eye can see I'm in bed with whooping cough, scarlet fever and hangnails."

Bud caught his breath, for obviously Gram had seen through Gramps' nonchalance. Normally there would have been more questions, but now Gram had something else on her mind. With a flourish, she plucked a letter from her apron pocket.

"From Helen!" she exclaimed. "She'll be here with Hal and the children on Christmas! Isn't that nice? With the other children and counting the grandchildren, there'll be at least thirty-three for Christmas!"

"Wonderful!" Gramps agreed. "Let's hope they stay more than just one day!"

"Helen Carruthers said she'll sleep the overflow if they do," Gram said. "With her children gone, too, and Joab in the hospital, she's lost in that big house. She told me so over the phone."

Gramps said firmly, "When our young'uns and their young'uns come home, they stay here."

The house would be spilling over with Bennetts, in-laws of Bennetts and grandchildren of Bennetts. Something within Bud turned stone cold and for a moment he wanted to die as he realized he did not have first claim or any real claim on the affections of these two people he had come to love so dearly. They had children of their own, natural children, and the fact that he was an orphan seemed more bitter to Bud than it ever had before. He felt it would have been better if he never had come here, for he had given his whole heart to Gram and Gramps who already had so many · that there couldn't possibly be room for one more.

Gram and Gramps began a happy discussion of the coming holiday. Helen Carruthers, who was so lonely anyway, would be glad to come in four or five days before Christmas to help Gram get ready. Naturally, Helen would leave on the twenty-fourth to spend

Christmas with Joab—and wasn't it a pity that he had had to be sent to a hospital almost two hundred miles from home when, if he was within reasonable distance, Helen could visit him so much oftener? But there would be plenty of help anyway. Gram hadn't raised her daughters without teaching them what to do in a kitchen.

Bud slipped out unobtrusively, and Shep followed him. As soon as they were hidden by a corner of the house, Bud hugged the collie fiercely. Then, with Shep beside him, he set off down the old tote road to find the black fawn.

The afternoon was waning when he returned, having seen five deer but not the black fawn. Although it was still early for chores, Bud cleaned the cow stable, fed and milked the four cows and took care of the milk. He looked to the horses and went to the chicken house, where this time he saw only the usual flock of mongrel chickens.

He collected the eggs from the nests and emerged from the chicken house to see Munn Mackie coming up the drive in his truck. A small building was chained securely onto the body of the truck. Gramps came from the house, buttoning his jacket as he came, and Munn stopped his truck.

"Where do you want her, Del?"

"Beside the hen house."

Munn's truck growled across the snow and came to a halt. Munn jumped from the cab, made a ramp of two-by-sixes and jockeyed the building onto the two-by-sixes until it skidded safely to the ground beside the hen house.

As Gramps paid Munn and the trucker drove away, Bud glanced at the little building beside the hen house. Until this afternoon he would have been eager to know why Munn had brought it and what it was for. Now he did not care.

"Shall we get the chores done?" Gramps asked.

"They're all done," Bud said.

THE SNOWPLOW PANTED AHEAD OF THE SCHOOL bus like a prehistoric monster. In some places there was only a dusting of snow and the plow raced along. In others there were drifts up to four feet deep, and the plow shifted into low gear and attacked the deep snow with its blade, growling like an angry dog attacking an enemy.

In a seat next to a window Bud studied the falling snow and could not help sharing in the excitement that had set in almost three weeks ago and had mounted ever since. The opening of the deer season was one of the major events of the year in Dishnoe County. Everybody who lived in the county and had a firearm was sure to be out that day and there would be many hunters from other places as well.

The Haleyville Consolidated School was not exempt from the influences of the season. Some boys from the fourth grade, more from the fifth and practically every boy from the sixth grade through high school would be absent on the opening day, and no excuse would be expected or required from them. Many of the girls would be out, too, and only a state law prevented the teachers from closing the school and joining their pupils in the cutover woods.

A surging bank of heavy clouds had covered the sky when Bud had left home in the morning. At noon a high wind had risen suddenly and snow had followed. Although only about four inches had fallen so far, the wind was making heavy drifts. Bud turned to his seatmate, a youngster who was tackling the complexities of the eighth grade for the third time. His name was Goethe Shakespeare Umberdehoven.

"Look at her come down, Get!"

"Yeah."

"There'll be tracking tomorrow."

"Yeah."

"You going out?"

"Yeah. We get a deer we can sell another pig and have more money."

This translation of getting a deer into financial terms was too much for Bud, who went back to staring at the snow. Soon only his physical self remained in the bus as his imagination took him into the deer woods with Gramps and the little thirty-thirty carbine Gramps had taught him to shoot. They were hot on the fresh trail of Old Yellowfoot and before long —by a clever ruse, the details of which Bud's imagination skipped over—they had outwitted the ruling monarch of Bennett's Woods. Knowing that there was no hope unless he ran, Old Yellowfoot raced away, eighteen feet to the jump, and Bud followed with his rifle. With the first shot Old Yellowfoot crumpled in the snow.

Then Bud heard the bus driver saying, "Hey, Sloan. You aim to get out in the next hour or so?"

Bud looked up to see that the bus was parked at the Bennett's drive. He squeezed past Get Umberdehoven and ran up the drive, stopping long enough to ruffle Shep's ears when he came bounding to meet him.

Daydreaming about Old Yellowfoot had made him feel better. The arrival of Gram and Gramps' children and grandchildren was as certain as the rising of the sun. Bud knew that they would displace him, for they belonged and he did not. But Christmas was not yet at hand and, maybe, if he wished hard enough, it never would come. Anyhow, there were at least the days before Christmas, and he decided to live for today and let tomorrow take care of itself.

In spite of the snow, Gramps was working on the little building that Munn Mackie had brought in his truck. Gramps had installed new and larger windows, put in insulation and rebuilt the door and hung it on new hinges. He was replacing some of the outside boards when Bud came up.

Bud asked no questions although now he wanted to. But he had ignored the building the day it was delivered, and pride prevented his asking about it now.

"By gummy," Gramps said over the blows of his hammer, which were strangely muffled in the storm, "sure looks as though we hit it right."

"We sure did," Bud agreed.

Gramps said solemnly, "Got the same feeling in

my bones as I had just before we caught Old Shark. Only this feeling's 'bout Old Yellowfoot. We'll nail him sure before the season's out."

"Gee! Are you sure?" Bud said, his reserve gone.

"Sure's a body can be 'thout putting it down on paper and swearing to it in front of Squire Sedlock. Yep. We're going to lay that old tyrant low."

"Gee!" Bud said again. "That'll be something! I'll run along and change."

"Come out when you're set if you've a mind to."

The storm-muffled thumps of Gramps' hammer were magic in Bud's ears as he ran around to the kitchen door, for in his imagination they had become rifle shots, widely spaced and well aimed, as Bud the master hunter once again maneuvered Old Yellowfoot into a corner from which there was no escape. Then he burst into the kitchen.

"Hi, Gram."

"Allan! I thought sure you'd be late, the way the wind's drifting this snow."

"We followed the snowplow up," Bud said, going to the table where his after-school snack always waited. He took a long drink of milk and a bite from a ginger cookie. "What's Gramps doing?"

"Trying to keep from driving himself and me too

crazy," Gram said, sniffing. "I do swear, he's more anxious than a boy on his first hunt! All day long he hasn't done much of anything except ask me if I think you'll get Old Yellowfoot. It's a good thing he's working it off."

Bud asked, "Do you think we'll get Old Yellowfoot?"

Gram smiled. "Let's put it this way. I think you'll have fun hunting him."

Bud finished the last cookie, drained the glass of milk, and sat silently for a moment. Then he asked a question that he had often been on the point of asking.

"Was Gramps ever kicked by a horse?"

"Land yes! Every farmer who uses horses has been kicked. At least, I never heard of one who hasn't."

"Was he ever kicked in the head?"

Gram laughed. "Lord love you, child. Who's been telling you fairy tales?"

"I just wondered."

Gram said dryly, "I've tended Delbert for a good many ailments but never yet, thank the Lord, for a horse-kicked head. What are you getting at, Allan?"

"I just sort of wondered," Bud said noncommittally.

He went up to his room more puzzled than ever. On the grouse hunt Gramps had said that a horse had kicked him in the head twenty-five years ago. But now Gram said there had never been any such kick, and Gram never lied. Still, if Gramps had not wanted her to worry after the grouse hunt, he had probably felt the same way twenty-five years ago. Perhaps he had never told her that he had been kicked in the head.

When Bud went out again, Gramps was in the cow stable and had already begun the milking. He was bubbling with enthusiasm. Gramps did everything with zest, but whenever there was anything exciting in prospect, he almost exploded with energy.

By the time they had finished the chores and eaten supper, Bud was almost giddy with excitement, for now the hour was at hand. He knew as he went to bed that he would never sleep a wink, but the next thing he knew Gramps was shaking his shoulder.

"Time to get moving, Bud."

It was dark outside, but that did not seem unusual because daylight did not come until after seven these days, and every morning for the past several weeks Bud had awakened in darkness. When he looked at his clock, however, he saw that it was a quarter to four. He sprang out of bed, instantly awake and exhilarated by the mere thought of starting anywhere at such an hour. But by the time he had reached the stable, Gramps had already milked three of the cows.

There was still only a faint hint of daylight when, the chores done, breakfast eaten and sack lunches in their jackets, they started into Bennett's Woods. Moored with a ten-foot hank of clothesline, Shep rolled his eyes and mournfully watched them go. Bud felt sorry for him until Gramps explained that, although most hunters are sportsmen, there are always a few who shoot first and look afterward. Two years ago some of that kind had shot one of Abel Carson's Holstein heifers, and said afterward that they thought it was a pinto buck. Since Shep liked to wander into the woods when there was nothing more interesting to do, it was better to leave him tied than to risk his being shot.

The snow had stopped falling, and here in the woods it had drifted less than in the open country where the wind had a full sweep. There were few drifts and no deep ones, and the five inches of soft snow made a pleasant cushion beneath Bud's pacs.

By almost imperceptible degrees the day lightened. They were perhaps a half mile from the house when Gramps stopped. He raised his rifle and sighted on a stump about a hundred yards away. Then he lowered his rifle and said, "We'll wait here a bit, Bud."

"Why?"

"It ain't light enough to see the sights, and while I think Old Yellowfoot will be hanging out in Dockerty's Swamp, he could be anywhere from here on. If we jump him, we don't want to guess where we're shooting."

Just then, they heard five shots.

"Fool!" Gramps growled. "He saw something move and, though it's a lead-pipe cinch he couldn't tell what it was, he shot anyway. Those kind of hunters got less brains than the game they hunt."

Twenty minutes later there were three more shots spaced far enough apart to indicate that the hunter was taking aim. Gramps listened carefully. He sighted a second time on the stump, held his sight for a full three seconds, and turned to Bud.

"What do you make of it?"

Bud raised his own rifle, centered the ivory bead of the front sight in the notched rear, and aimed at a puff of snow that clung like a boll of cotton to the stump. He lowered the rifle.

"It looks all right to me."

"You can see?"

"Well enough for a good aim."

"Come on, and from here on there's no talking."

Gramps slowed to a snail's pace, stopping every ten minutes or so to look all around. Bud understood what he was doing, for while it is true that deer are noted for their speed, it is a mistake to try to chase them. If you slog as far as twenty miles a day through deer country, you are almost sure to see deer, but not as many as the hunter who works carefully through a comparatively limited deer cover. Slow and easy is the proper way nine times out of ten.

Rifles were cracking from all quarters now, sometimes three or four at once, sometimes only one and occasionally none at all. Gramps stopped suddenly and pointed to two deer about a hundred and twenty yards away. Both were bucks. One bore a stunted rack of antlers, but the second had a trophy that would shame no hunter.

Gramps went on. The two bucks, aware now of their presence, each sounded a single blasting snort and bounded away. Bud watched them go without regret. Either buck would have been a fairly simple shot. But they were hunting Old Yellowfoot.

They saw seven more deer before they reached Dockerty's Swamp. It covered about seventy acres and was a tangle of high bush huckleberries, cedar, balsam and a few great hardwoods, whose branches rose gaunt and bare above the surrounding stunted growth. A bush-grown knoll flanked the swamp and it was surrounded by low mountains that were covered with cutover hardwoods and patches of laurel and small evergreens. Although Dockerty's Swamp was well known as a refuge for deer, Gramps was one of the few who knew how to flush them out.

Gramps led Bud to the summit of the knoll and halted in a thicket so dense that they could see no farther than forty feet ahead of them. Gramps raised a forefinger, a signal for Bud to stay where he was. Foolish young deer might show themselves in sparse cover or even open meadows, but a buck as wise as Old Yellowfoot would make for the thickest cover when Gramps chased him out of the swamp. It was a foregone conclusion that he would come up the knoll. All other ways out of the swamp were so sparsely forested that anything emerging would make an easy shot.

Two and a half hours after Gramps left, Bud saw a deer move farther down the slope. Bud remained perfectly still. The deer was almost completely hidden by brush and he was unable to tell if it was a buck or doe or even how large it was.

Ten seconds later the black fawn stepped into plain sight.

He was a well-grown buck now, and sturdy, and his hair was so dark that the fawn spots had faded into it. Little nubbins that were his first antlers projected two inches above his head.

The black buck came on, stopping now and then to look behind him and always testing the winds. He had been chased from the swamp and, young though he was, he had planned and executed a masterly retreat instead of panicking. He passed thirty feet to Bud's right, turned and stared fixedly at him when they were abreast. Then the black buck leaped out of sight into a laurel thicket.

Three does came next, then a chesty little six-point buck that shook his antlers and rolled his eyes as though anything that dared challenge him did so at its own peril. Finally Gramps appeared.

"Old Yellowfoot wasn't there, Bud. We'll try Happy Ridge."

But Old Yellowfoot was not on Happy Ridge, or in Hargen's Pines or Dead Man's Hollow, or any other place where they looked. They might have had either one of two more nice bucks that day, but they scorned both.

Finally, sorry that a nearly perfect day was ending, Gramps and Bud turned homeward. Tomorrow was another day and there were more to follow. They entered the house and Gramps said to Gram,

"Nary a sign, not even an old track . . ."

He stopped suddenly, staggered across the floor and dropped his rifle on the table before sinking into a chair. He buried his face in his hands, and once more Bud heard the terrible wheezing that had been so terrifying back in the grouse woods.

chapetr 7

From the school bus the blacktop road looked to Bud like a frozen black river between the banks of snow cast aside by the snow-plow and he pretended that the poles indicating culverts were channel markers. The Barston farm buildings to the left and a hundred and fifty yards from the highway seemed to him an island in the sea of snow and the Barstons' orchard looked like a great mass of seaweed.

Soon he tired of daydreaming and stared stonily out of the window. When Christmas had still been weeks

116

away, he had been able to tell himself that it might never come. But now that only a few days remained before Christmas, there was no more hope. This was the last trip the school bus would be making until after New Year's, for the Christmas vacation was beginning and in just three days Gram and Gramps' children and grandchildren would arrive and there would be no place for an outsider.

It would have been far better, he thought bleakly, if he had never come to Bennett's Farm and probably it would be better if he left now. But although Bud's imagination could whisk him anywhere at all, the harsh realities of life as he had lived it sobered him. He could dream of the French Foreign Legion, the carefree existence of a cowboy, the adventurous career of a seaman or the unhampered life of a trapper in the arctic north, but he knew in his heart his dreams would never come true. Twelve-year-old boys had run away from the orphanage, but none had stayed away for more than three days before they had returned of their own accord or had been brought back by the police. A youngster traveling alone without resources had less than one chance in a thousand of remaining undetected, and Bud knew it.

Besides, he was stubborn and unwilling to back away

from any situation. He would face the assembled Bennetts and do the best he could. In one way or another, he had faced giants before.

To take his mind away from the ordeal ahead of him, Bud turned back to the hunt for Old Yellowfoot and the day Gramps had been stricken in the kitchen.

He had been frightened then, too, but not with the stark fear he had known the day he and Gramps had hunted for grouse and Gramps had become ill while they were in the woods. That day Bud had been alone, but now there was Gram. Things might still go wrong now, but not altogether wrong if she was there.

He remembered how Gram had walked calmly over to Gramps as soon as he was stricken and said quietly,

"You're tired, Delbert. Now you just sit right there and take it easy."

Then she had gone to the telephone and, after she had spoken to Dr. Beardsley, returned to sit beside Gramps. Only her eyes had shown the torment she was enduring. Bud had hovered in the background, not knowing what to do, but ready to do anything. Gramps raised his head again and there was that terrible convulsive cough, but afterward he breathed more easily. The blue color that had invaded his face began to fade. He started to sweat and Gram wiped his face gently.

"Gosh blame nonsense," Gramps gasped.

"Of course," Gram said. "That's just what it is. You sit there anyway."

"Why?"

"Maybe because I like your company and you have been gone all day."

Only later had it occurred to Bud that she was deliberately resorting to subterfuge to make him sit still until Dr. Beardsley arrived. Gramps would never have accepted a doctor otherwise. As it was, he gave an outraged growl when Dr. Beardsley finally came.

"What the blazes do you want?" Gramps grumbled.

Dr. Beardsley said calmly, "To see you, Delbert, and I don't have all night. Open your shirt."

Dr. Beardsley had hung out his shingle in Haleyville when he was twenty-two. He was seventy-two now, and there was little in his half century of practice that he hadn't dealt with. He had learned long ago that he would be obeyed if he expected obedience and tolerated nothing else.

"While you're about it," the doctor said, "roll up your sleeve."

Grumbling, Gramps did as he was told. Dr. Beardsley took his blood pressure and thrust a thermometer between Gramps' lips. When Gramps made a face, he said,

"That's a thermometer, Delbert, not a stick of peppermint. Don't try to bite it in half."

While Gramps mouthed the thermometer, Dr. Beardsley applied a stethoscope to his chest, then to his back. He removed the thermometer and, after he read it, he washed it at the sink and dipped it in a sterile tube before putting it back in its case.

"I suppose you were hunting today?" he asked Gramps.

"You know anybody who wasn't?" Gramps said.

"I know some who shouldn't have been, and I know at least one who isn't going again until next year. His name's Delbert Bennett."

"Blasted nonsense!" Gramps snorted. "You doctors ever talk anything 'cept nonsense?"

"Seldom," Dr. Beardsley admitted cheerfully, "but it just so happens that I'm talking sense at present. It isn't too serious, but it will be if you don't take care. The truth is your heart isn't as young as it used to be. With reasonable luck it will last you another twenty years, and I fully expect you'll grow more cussed every year. But right now it needs rest, which means that you're going to take it easy for the next six months. In addition to your regular night's sleep, lie down for at least three hours every day. We'll see after that."

"I never heard so blame much foolishness!" Gramps tried to roar, but he was too weak and could only blink indignantly at Dr. Beardsley.

Gram said quietly but firmly, "He'll do as you say, Doctor."

"Clobber him if he doesn't."

"I will."

Dr. Beardsley packed his stethoscope and sphygmomanometer back in his bag and wrote a prescription, which he handed to Gram.

"There's no emergency about this; the youngster can bring it when he comes home from school tomorrow. After that, see that he takes his medicine according to the directions that will accompany the prescription and refill it before it runs out."

"Medicine!" Gramps said. "You pill peddlers can't think of anything else when you don't know what to do."

"He'll take the medicine, Doctor," Gram promised.

Dr. Beardsley said, "I leave you in care of your boss,

Delbert," and went out into the night.

That had been that; hunting Old Yellowfoot was over for the season. Gramps grumbled and growled, but he took his medicine and accepted his three hours of daily rest. Bud shouldered as many of the chores as he could.

Then the school bus stopped, and as Bud trudged up the drive, he told himself sullenly that at least he was beholden to nobody for he had paid his way. But in his heart he knew it wasn't as simple as that, and that he would gladly work as many hours a day as he could stay awake to help Gram and Gramps.

For the past week the kitchen had been a heaven of tantalizing odors. Bushels of cookies and rows of fruit cakes had emerged from the great oven. Gram and Helen Carruthers had been busy from daylight until after dark. Gram was taking another tray of cookies from the oven when Bud came in and she smiled at him. Helen Carruthers, a tall, graying woman who seldom smiled, was mixing something in a pan. She nodded at Bud and told him to help himself.

Bud grabbed a handful of cookies and went to his room to change his clothes. As he went out to the barn, Shep came running to meet him and inside he found Gramps sitting on a bale of hay. The barn had become Gramps' refuge. The old man nodded glumly.

"Dogged if I know how she does it," Gramps said plaintively. "I'm supposed to take that stuff Doc Beardsley gave me, and it's a wonder it don't kill a body, every four hours. So every four hours, no matter how busy she is, Mother's right on deck with it. Pah! A man can't be himself any more."

"You should have your medicine, Gramps."

"Medicine, yes, but that ain't any medicine. Now you take sassafras root and slippery elm bark; that was medicine when they was boiled together by somebody who knew what he was doing." Gramps fell into a glum silence. Then he said, "Anyhow, they didn't get Old Yellowfoot."

"How do you know?"

"Everybody'd know if they got a buck that big. He'll be waiting for us next year."

"That's good!" Bud said with feeling.

"Ain't it," Gramps said sourly. "It'd be a heap better if next deer season wasn't such a passeling ways off. I felt in my bones that this was our year to get Old Yellowfoot, and we'd of had him if it hadn't been for this blasted nonsense. Oh well, we'll be howling a long spell if we howl about it. Want to help me fetch the Christmas tree tomorrow?"

THE NEXT DAY THEY SET OFF ACROSS THE SNOW with Shep frolicking beside them. Bud carried an ax and a rope. Gramps led the way to a young hemlock that, because it grew in the open, was evenly formed on all sides and sloped to a nearly perfect top. Bud felled it, then hitched the rope around its trunk and slid it home across the snow. Under Gramps' direction he sawed the chopped end off squarely and nailed a wooden standard across the trunk. Gram and Helen Carruthers took over as soon as Gramps and Bud had carried the tree into the living room and stood it in a corner. The tree had to be moved this way and that, seldom more than two inches in any direction, until Gram and Helen were finally satisfied and the top could be secured with string.

Even while he was helping with the Christmas preparations, Bud felt detached. He was convinced that they were being made solely for the Bennetts' children and grandchildren, in whose eyes he would be no more than an interloper. And so Bud walked grudgingly forward when the first of the real family arrived, forcing himself not to surrender to an impulse to run. As soon as he had mumbled "Pleased t'meetcha," he fled to the barn.

By Christmas morning the house was filled with Bennett relatives and more would be there in time for dinner. It was still dark when Bud awakened, and he slipped quietly out of bed and into his clothes. Then, shoes in hand, he padded softly down the stairs. He wanted to escape from the house and be out with the stock. Also, Gramps needed rest, and if he were not disturbed, he would sleep late enough so that Bud could finish the chores. Otherwise, Gramps would insist on helping. Bud knew by the light seeping through the crack under the kitchen door that somebody had preceded him. It was Gram.

"Allan," she said, "it's only half-past five."

She must have been up for a very long time. Now she was filling the last of a row of pies. As he watched her, Bud could not help thinking of the feast to come —roast turkey, chicken, duck and goose; sweet and white potatoes; mince, pumpkin and apple pie; salads and cooked vegetables; cake and ice cream. But he refused to look into the dining room, where the big table had been extended to its full length and been flanked by many small tables. There would be more than thirty at Christmas dinner, and there was room and food for all of them.

Bud was just as careful to avoid the parlor where gifts were piled in little mountains beneath the tree. He thought fleetingly of the sewing kit he had put under the tree for Gram and the book called *Africa's Dangerous Game* for Gramps. Without resentment, he reflected that there would be nothing for him.

He put on his shoes and took his jacket and cap from the closet, and was about to go out when he saw that he was being rude to Gram. Even if Christmas meant nothing to him, it meant a great deal to her. And so he turned and wished her a Merry Christmas as heartily as he could.

"Why bless you, Allan. And a very Merry Christmas to you," she said, hugging and kissing him. Even though he had no claim on Gram, it looked as if she had not rejected him completely, and he felt a little better.

He left the house and stopped on the back porch to hug Shep, whose warm, wet tongue seemed to wash away some of Bud's loneliness. Together they made their way through the snow to the stable where the four cows, warm in their stanchions, blew softly through their nostrils and turned their gently welcoming eyes on Bud. Some farmers claimed cows were glad to see you only because you gave them food, but Bud knew better, especially on this Christmas morning.

He forked hay into the mangers, measured grain into the feed boxes and drew his stool up beside the fractious Cherub. It seemed a long while ago and scarcely credible that he had once been afraid of her.

Bud milked the four cows deliberately, working as slowly as possible so as to delay his return to the house in which he had become an alien. Then he fed the horses, took care of the chickens and peered out of the barn at the winter landscape which was gradually becoming lighter. Although he had already cleaned it once, he cleaned the cow stable again, carefully sifting anything that even remotely resembled refuse from the fresh straw he had put down and carrying the refuse out to the litter pile behind the barn.

He lingered on in the barn until he knew that if he did not return to the house Gram or Gramps would come out to find out what had happened to him. They would want to know what was the matter, and he was determined not to spoil their happiness at Christmas by letting them know how miserable he was.

As soon as he was inside the kitchen, Bud took off his work shoes and put on the pair he wore to school. It was an involuntary and almost unconscious gesture. He and Gramps always came to the table in the shoes they wore in the barn, and as long as they were clean, neither of them gave it a second thought. But now the house was full of strangers.

Only Gram seemed to notice his entrance and she came into the kitchen from the dining room where the others were and started to cook his bacon and eggs.

"Land sake, Allan, you were a long while at the chores," she said.

Bud stayed in the kitchen with her, hoping that he would be able to eat there alone. But when his breakfast was ready, she carried the plate into the dining room and Bud set his jaw and followed.

He had no sooner sat down than Gramps came in. He nodded at the table in general and then turned to Bud.

"Did you do the morning chores, young feller?"

Bud said, "Yes," in a very small voice.

"Did you get into that little house, too?"

128

"Little house?"

"The one next the chicken house."

"No."

"You'd best kite along and get it."

Bud left the table, glad to get away, but burning with humiliation. The little house that Munn Mackie had hauled in with his truck had nothing in it. At least Bud thought it had nothing in it. But having been too proud to ask about it in the beginning or since, he wasn't sure now. In spite of all his precautions, he had come close to saddling Gramps with a chore that he, Bud, ought to have done without Gramps' having to ask him.

Bud came to the little house and, seeing a white envelope tied with a red ribbon to the door latch, stood dumfounded. "*Merry Christmas*" was written across the envelope and the card inside it read:

Merry Christmas to our boy, Bud-Allan.
Gram and Gramps

Bud opened the door and gasped. Last night after he had gone to bed somebody must have strewn fresh straw on the floor of the little house. There was a drinking fountain, a mash hopper, a grain feeder and a container for oyster shell. A regal young cockerel strutted around six pure-white pullets.

Bud entered the little house and pulled the door shut behind him, latching it so no one could intrude on this wonderful moment. His heart seemed to be beating in his throat and tears had sprung to his eyes. Now for the first time in his life he knew what Christmas could mean.

He caught up the cockerel and, as he stroked it, looked around at the pullets and thought of the flock they would become.

Bud was sure he had always wanted White Wyandottes like these.

chapter   8

G RAMPS TOOK A TURN
for the better soon after the Christmas guests de-
parted, but his improvement was not an unmitigated
blessing. The better he felt, the more his enforced
confinement chafed. Sores that were opened because
he had to stop hunting Old Yellowfoot after only one
day were rubbed raw because he could not go into
the winter woods at all. There was little he could have
done there if he had gone, but he still fretted to go.

He read and reread *Africa's Dangerous Game*, the
book Bud had given him for Christmas, and criticized

each chapter as he read it. The book was the abridged journal of an obscure professional hunter, and Gramps had no sympathy at all for the hardships the author had suffered or the perils he had faced. After all, Gramps said, he didn't have to go looking for rogue elephants, man-killing lions or short-tempered buffalo. And since he had gone after them of his own free will, he should have known about the perils he would have to face before he had ever started out. Of course he could expect trouble—what hunter couldn't?—but the book would have been far more interesting if he had given more space to hunting and less to the unendurable agonies that had beset him. In fact, Gramps thought the long chapter in which the hunter crossed the desert might better have been condensed into a single sentence reading, "Don't cross this desert unless you carry plenty of water."

Although the stature of the hero of *Africa's Dangerous Game* dwindled with each perusal, reading was a way to help ease the long hours when Gramps could do little. And so Bud brought home books from the school library. Usually he chose books with outdoor themes, and instead of taking them to his room, he purposely left them on the kitchen table where Gramps would see them. Gramps was always volubly critical and often openly scornful of the books Bud brought home for him, but he read them all.

When he was not reading or helping with the chores if Bud had not managed to get them all done, Gramps devised endless cunning schemes for getting the best of Old Yellowfoot next season. For Old Yellowfoot, his one failure, galled Gramps every bit as much as Sir Lancelot would have been galled had he been un-horsed by a downy-cheeked young squire. The fact that illness had given Gramps only one day to hunt Old Yellowfoot did not worry him. All that mattered was that Old Yellowfoot still wore the rack of antlers that Gramps had sworn to hang in the living room.

Although the next deer season was still months away, Gramps gave his campaign all the care and at-tention an able general would lavish on a crucial bat-tle. He carried a map of Bennett's Woods in his head and time after time his imagination took him through every thicket in which the great buck might hide. He pondered ways to drive him out and the various countermoves Old Yellowfoot might make to try to elude him. Gramps made lists, not only of the ways in which Old Yellowfoot could be expected to behave differently from young and relatively inexperienced deer, but also of his individual traits.

One evening in early April Bud read one of the lists that Gramps had left on the kitchen table:

Old Yellowfoot knows more about hunters than they do about him.

He will not be spooked and he cannot be driven.

Don't expect to find him where such a buck might logically be found, but don't overlook hunting him there. He does the unexpected.

If the weather's mild, look for him in the heights, especially Hagerman's Knob, Eagle Hill and Justin's Bluff.

If there's plenty of snow, he'll be in the lowlands. (Though I've yet to find him in Dockerty's Swamp during deer season, Bud and me will look for him there.)

Old Yellowfoot's one of the very few deer I've ever run across who's smart enough to work against the wind instead of running before it. I'm sure he does this the better to locate hunters.

Hunt thickets close to farms. I've a hunch he's hung out in them more than once while we looked for him in the deep woods.

He will never cross an open space if he can help it, and he always can.

Then glancing once more at the list, Bud returned to his own figuring. He frowned and nibbled the eraser of his pencil as he looked at the sheets of paper scattered on the table in front of him, and finally arranged them in a neat sheaf and started over them again.

He knew pretty well what Gram and Gramps had paid for his pen of White Wyandottes, and the price was high. They were the best chickens that could be bought and, in terms of what they would bring in the market, the cockerel was worth any two dozen run-of-the-mill chickens and each of the pullets was worth any dozen. But expensive as the White Wyandottes had been, so far they had been anything but a bonanza.

Fed according to a formula worked out by Bud and the agriculture teacher at the Haleyville Consolidated School, the pullets had averaged more eggs for each bird than the pullets in Gramps' flock, and the cost of feeding them had been less. But Bud's pleasure at this proof that scientifically fed chickens did more for less money was somewhat diminished by the fact that until the past few weeks his chickens had produced only undersized pullets' eggs. When he accepted such eggs at all, Pat Haley would never pay more than twenty-seven cents a dozen. Gram used the surplus eggs in cooking, and Bud had taken his pay in feed rather than cash. He still owed Gramps sixty-nine cents for feed, and even though Gramps had told him not to worry, Bud couldn't help it, for after wintering his flock he was sixty-nine cents in debt, and now there were fresh problems.

Since it was unthinkable to let his aristocrats mingle with the farm flock, a run was necessary. Bud could cut the supporting posts in Bennett's Woods, but wire netting cost money. Besides, there would be no more income from egg sales for some time, for now that the six pullets had begun to lay normal-sized eggs, every one of the eggs had to be hoarded against the time when one or more of the six turned broody. To prove that there was more profit in better chickens, Bud had to increase his flock. The arguments for incubators as opposed to the time-honored setting hen were reasonable but it was out of the question for Bud to buy even a small incubator. And so, although he could expect no income from egg sales, at least for a while, he was still faced with the problem of building a run and of feeding his flock.

It was true that the future looked bright. Something like half the chicks hatched would probably be cockerels and the other half pullets. The rooster Bud already had would serve very well for several years more and the little house could comfortably accommodate him and about twenty hens. If the overflow were sold . . .

"What's the matter, Bud?" Gramps interrupted. "You look as though you just dug yourself a fourteen-foot hole, crawled in, and pulled the hole in on top of you."

Bud shook himself out of the reverie into which he had lapsed and looked up to see Gramps standing across the table. Bud grinned. There was something like the old sparkle in Gramps' eye and his chin had its old defiant tilt.

"I owe you sixty-nine cents for chicken feed, Gramps," Bud said, looking back at his figures.

"Serious matter," Gramps said gravely. "But I promise not to have the sheriff attach your flock if you pay in the next day or so. If you're dead set on having that worry off your mind, why don't you sell some eggs?"

"I'm saving them for hatching."

"Can't save your eggs and pay your debts, too," Gramps pointed out. "How many you got laid by?"

"Forty-four."

"Pat Haley'll buy 'em, and now that your hens have started laying something bigger'n robin's eggs, he'll pay better. You can pay me off and still have forty, fifty cents for yourself."

Bud looked at the old man. Sometimes he knew how to take Gramps, but this time he wasn't sure. "I have to save them," he said.

"You don't have to do anything of the kind," Gramps said. "If you're saving eggs it's 'cause you want to, and if you want to, it's 'cause you got something in mind. You aim to hatch those eggs?"

"Yes. I think the little house will hold maybe twenty hens and a rooster."

" 'Bout right," Gramps conceded. "So you have seven in there now and forty-four eggs saved. If you get an eighty per cent hatch, and that won't be bad for a rooster as don't yet know too much 'bout his business, you'll have thirty-five more chickens. So that makes forty-two in a twenty-one hen house. It don't add up."

Bud said quickly, "That isn't what I have in mind. I'll keep fourteen of the best pullets and sell all the rest."

"Something in that," Gramps admitted. "Pat Haley'll pay you the going price for both fryers and broilers. Take out the cost of feed, and if you're lucky, come fall you could have ten or fifteen dollars for yourself."

Bud said thoughtfully, "I hadn't meant to sell any for fryers. I'd hoped to sell the surplus as breeding stock."

"Hope is the most stretchable word in the dictionary," Gramps said. "If we didn't have it we'd be better off dead but there's such a thing as having too much. Many a man who's tried to live on hope alone has ended up with both hands full of nothing. Do you think anybody who knows anything about poultry will pay you breeding-stock prices for chickens from an untried pen?"

"But my chickens have the best blood lines there are," Bud said.

"And it don't mean a blasted thing unless they have a lot of what it takes," Gramps said. "Joe Barston paid seven hundred and fifty dollars for a four-month-old bull calf whose ancestors had so much blue blood they all but wore monocles. But this calf threw the measliest lot of runts you ever saw and finally Joe sold him for beef. Now if you had a proven pen of chickens, if you could show in black and white that yours produced the most meat and laid the most eggs for the breed, you could sell breeding stock. Otherwise you're out of luck." Gramps shrugged.

Bud stared dully at his papers. Dreaming of getting ten dollars or more for a cockerel that was worth a dollar and thirty-five cents as a broiler had been just another ride on a pink cloud, and his dreams of wealth in the fall evaporated.

"Your chin came close to fracturing your big toe," Gramps said. "Don't be licked before you are. Now you don't want to keep your own pullets 'cause you'll be breeding daughters back to their own father, and that's not for you. At least, it's not until you know more about such things. But you can trade some of yours back to the same farm where your pen came from. He'll probably ask more than bird for bird, but he'll trade and the least you can figure on is starting out this fall with a bigger flock. The rest you'd better figure on selling to Joe Haley. Now how many eggs have you been getting a day?"

"The least I've had since spring weather set in is two. The most is five."

"That's all? You never got six?"

"Not yet."

"Have you tried trap-nesting your hens?"

"No."

"Why not?"

Bud knew that trapping each hen in her nest after she laid and keeping a record of her production was the only way to weed out the drones from the workers. He hadn't tried it, though, because he hadn't wanted to leave any hen trapped away from food and water while he was at school all day. He hadn't wanted to ask Gramps to look after his trap nests for him either, but he only said lamely, "I never thought of it."

"You should have," Gramps said. "If you're going to make out with these hifalutin' chickens of yours you have to think of everything. Looks to me like you got a slacker in your flock and, though maybe she wouldn't be better off in the stew pot, you'd be better off to put her there."

"That's so," Bud conceded, "but how do I know which one?"

"You don't and there's no sense fussing about it now. So what else is bothering you?"

"I haven't got any money," Bud confessed.

"That," Gramps' serious eyes seemed suddenly to twinkle, "puts you in the same boat with forty-nine million and two other people. Why do you need money?"

"I need to build an enclosed run. I can't let my chickens run with the farm flock."

"True," Gramps said. "High society chickens oughtn't mix with ordinary fowl. Why don't you go ahead and build your run?"

"I told you. I haven't any money for netting and staples."

"Go in that little room beside the granary and you'll find a role of netting. Kite yourself down to Pat Haley's during lunch hour tomorrow, get some staples, and tell Pat to charge 'em to me."

"But . . ."

"Will you let me finish?" Gramps said sharply. "I didn't say you were going to get any part of it for free. That roll of netting cost me four dollars and sixty cents. Add to it whatever the staples cost, and since you want to save your eggs for hatching, somebody's got to buy feed for your chickens. I'll take you on until you have fryers to sell, but strictly as a business deal. Just a minute."

Gramps wrote on a sheet of paper, shoved it across the table, and Bud read,

> On demand I promise to pay to Delbert J. Bennett the sum of ———. My pen of White Wyandottes plus any increase therefrom shall be security for the payment of this note.

Bud looked inquiringly across the table. Gramps shrugged. "All you have to do is sign it and go ahead;

you're in the chicken business if you want in."

"How much will I owe you?"

"I'll fill in the amount when the time comes," Gramps promised. "Do you want to sign or don't you?"

"I'll sign," Bud said, and painfully he wrote *Allan Wilson Sloan* in the proper place and gave the note back to Gramps.

The old man was folding it in his wallet when Gram said, "What nonsense is this?" She had come into the kitchen unnoticed and plainly she had been observing Gramps and Bud for some time. Her face was stormier than Bud had ever seen it and her normally gentle eyes snapped. Nonchalantly Gramps tucked the wallet into his pocket.

"Just a little business deal, Mother. I'm going to finance Bud's chicken business and he's going to pay me back when he sells his broilers and fryers."

"The idea," Gram said. "The very idea. Give that note back at once, Delbert Bennett."

"Now don't get all het up, Mother. A deal's a deal."

Bud saw that Gram's fury was beginning to touch Gramps in a tender spot, and he fidgeted nervously and said,

143

"I'd rather have it this way, Gram."

Gram answered by glaring at Gramps and flouncing out of the room. Bud looked dismally after her and turned to Gramps with a feeble smile.

"She shouldn't be so upset. I don't want anyone except me to pay for my chickens."

"She'll be a long while mad 'less she gets over it," Gramps said, still smarting. "Anything else, Bud?"

"Yes. How many eggs can you put under a setting hen?"

"Depends on the size of the hen. A small one'll take eleven, a medium-size can handle thirteen and you can put fifteen 'neath a big hen."

"When do you think my hens will turn broody?"

"Hard telling," Gramps growled. "A hen's a female critter and when it comes to doing anything sensible they ain't no different from other female critters. Hell and high water can't make 'em do anything 'thout they put their mind to it, and nine cases of dynamite can't stop 'em once they do."

Two days later, when he had carried five more eggs to his hoard that now numbered forty-seven, Bud found only two eggs left. He was sure that Gram or Gramps had mistakenly sent the eggs he had been saving to Haleyville along with the regular farm shipment. He went sadly out to the barn where Gramps was going over his gardening tools.

"You look like you'd swallowed a quart of vinegar," the old man said as he glanced up.

"It isn't that," Bud said forlornly. "Somebody sent most of my hatching eggs to market."

"No they didn't," Gramps said. "Three of my hens went broody and I took 'em. Put fifteen eggs under each, seeing they were big hens."

"But they're your hens."

"Don't trouble your head," Gramps said. "Setting hen rent'll be on the bill when time comes to settle up."

THE FOLLOWING AUTUMN, WHEN BUD HAD BEEN at Gram and Gramps' for more than a year, he strode down a tote road into Bennett's Woods with Shep tagging at his heels. Bright red and yellow leaves waved on every hardwood and swished underfoot as he plowed through them. The evergreens were ready for the frigid blasts to come, and the laurel and rhododendrons, touched but never daunted by frost, rattled in the sharp north wind.

A gray squirrel, frantically harvesting nuts and seeds before deep snow came, scooted up a tree, flattened himself on a limb and chirred when Bud went past. Three grouse rose on rattling wings. A sleek doe snorted and, curling her white tail over her back, bounded away.

Bud was oblivious, for he had come into Bennett's Woods to try to solve the problems that were bedeviling him.

That summer he had succeeded in hatching seventy-nine chicks. Seventy-four had survived, a far better percentage than was average, because Bud had watched his flock constantly for disease, predators and accidents.

The poultryman from whom Gram and Gramps had bought the original stock had traded fourteen young pullets for fourteen of Bud's pullets and three of Bud's cockerels, with Bud paying express charges both ways. The rest Bud had sold to Pat Haley. After paying Gramps every penny he owed him and interest as well, Bud had $8.97 to show for his summer's toil, and his problems were not yet ended. For even after they started to lay, it would be a long while before his pullets would produce full-sized eggs.

146

Shep curled up beside him on the bank of Skunk Creek as Bud sat there and stared moodily at the stream wondering how he would see his increased flock through the winter with only $8.97 and perhaps some egg money.

All he wanted from life was to stay on the farm with Gram and Gramps. He knew he would never even be well off if he reckoned success in financial terms alone, but the whirr of a winging grouse, the snort of a deer and the leap of a trout meant more to him than money, and he knew they always would. Still dreams have to have a practical side, too. Even if money is the root of all evil, it is indispensable, and Bud thought again of the $8.97 that he had earned that summer.

Suddenly he froze in his place. Back in the trees across the creek he saw a flicker. Then the black buck appeared. Bud sat spellbound, recalling the day when, heartsick and lonely, he had ventured into the woods and found a brother in the black buck. The buck now came cautiously down to the creek and Bud's eyes widened with delight.

Although this was his first year, the black buck was as big as some of the two- and three-year-old bucks that Bud and Gramps had seen in the woods.

And instead of the spikes or fork horn that young bucks usually have, the black buck had a very creditable pair of antlers with three symmetrical tines on each. The buck drank and then, raising his dripping muzzle, caught Bud's scent and raced back into the woods.

Bud rose and started homeward, his depression gone. The black buck had faced his problems, too, and many of them had surely been desperate. But he had triumphed magnificently. This made Bud feel better and to see that his own situation was far brighter than he had thought. For although he had very little cash, he had more than tripled his flock. Moreover, he had the run and he owed nothing. Best of all he had the future.

chapter 9

Oɴᴇ ᴡɪɴᴛᴇʀ ᴀғᴛᴇʀ-
noon during his third year with Gram and Gramps,
Bud was waiting in the study hall for Mr. Demarest,
who taught agriculture at the Haleyville High School.
Bud glanced at the clock on the wall. What seemed
an hour ago it had been five minutes past four. Now it
was only six minutes after. He sighed and stared out
at the snow that was trampled in the yards and left in
dirty piles in the street.

Winter always seemed a barren, meaningless season
in Haleyville. At Bennett's Farm, however, where the

snow covered the fields with an inviting blanket and transformed the woods into another world, winter was a natural and fitting part of things. There the seasons were fully seen and felt, not mere dates on a calendar as they were in town. Spring was the time for new life to be born, summer for spring-born life to attain maturity, autumn for the harvest to be gathered and winter for the land to rest and recuperate for spring.

As he stared out the study-hall window, Bud thought of Bennett's Woods, where Old Yellowfoot still bore his proud rack of antlers as he skulked through the thickets and tested the wind for signs of an enemy. He had been unmolested for the past two seasons, for Gramps had not been well enough to hunt deer and nobody else had a chance of hunting him successfully.

In Bennett's Woods, too, the black buck, now a king in his own right, snorted his challenge from the ridges and put to flight lesser bucks that sought the favor of the does he coveted. Three years had not dimmed Bud's memory of his first meeting with the tiny black fawn or lessened his feeling of bondship with him. Whenever Bud was troubled or faced with problems for which there seemed to be no solution, he still went into Bennett's Woods to seek out the black buck. And always he found there the answer he needed, for seeing the black buck achieve his destiny gave Bud the confidence he needed to work out his own life.

Some of the things that had happened before he came to Bennett's Farm now seemed as remote as if they had taken place during some other life. Bud could hardly believe that he had been the frightened, defiant twelve-year-old boy who had trudged up the Bennetts' driveway three years ago expecting nothing and having received everything. It seemed incredible that three years had elapsed since then and that he had gone on from grammar school into high school. And although his marks were not the highest in his class, they were still a source of pride to Gram and Gramps.

Some of the things that had seemed horribly unreal, Bud now saw in their true perspective. He remembered vividly his first Christmas at the farm, but now he knew and liked the Bennetts' children and grandchildren. And now he appreciated the true measure of his own love for Gram and Gramps. He had been a starved waif, and they had fed his soul as well as his body. More than ever he wanted to be with them always, to live as they had lived and to shape his life by the ideals to which they had clung. But to be as good a farmer as Gramps had been, Bud needed technical knowledge. That was why he was waiting for Mr. Demarest.

Bud thought wistfully of Gramps, who for the past two seasons had been forced to confine his outdoor activities to a little fishing and grouse hunting. But now he was fit again, and when the deer season opened tomorrow, he and Bud would be on the trail of Old Yellowfoot once more. This time they were certain to bag him; Gramps felt it in his bones.

Then the door opened and Mr. Demarest came in. He was a small man, but quick and wiry. He was in his late thirties, but the ordeals of a poverty-stricken boyhood and youth had made him look ten years older than he was. His black hair had gray streaks and he could never manage more than a fleeting smile. The son of a ne'er-do-well tenant farmer, Mr. Demarest had had no formal schooling until he was fifteen. But then he had set doggedly out to educate himself. Once he had done so, he had dedicated himself to teaching future farmers how to succeed, for he could not forget his father's many failures.

"I'm sorry to be late, Allan," he said pleasantly as he came through the study-hall door. "What's on your mind, son?"

"Mr. Demarest," Bud stammered, "I want to be a farmer."

"Is something stopping you?" Mr. Demarest's eyes twinkled.

"No," Bud said. "I'm certain I can throw in with Gramps Bennett and take over from him. I can buy out Gram and Gramps' children. They aren't interested in farming."

"Think it over carefully," Mr. Demarest said seriously. "There are better farms you might have."

"I don't want any other farm," Bud said firmly. "I want that one."

"It's sort of special, eh?"

"It's very special."

"Then what is your problem?"

"I don't know enough," Bud said. "Three years ago, for Christmas, I was given a pen of White Wyandottes. They're the Eichorn strain, about as good as you can get. I built from them and I was able to show Gramps that my purebreds were more profitable than his mongrel flock. We replaced his flock with Eichorn Wyandottes, too, and we're doing all right with them. But I can see where I made a lot of mistakes that needn't have been made if I had known how to avoid them. I want to go to college and study agriculture."

"Do you have any money?"

"No," Bud said. "I'm going to need most of what I have saved for berry plants next spring."

"But why, if you've built up a flock of Eichorn Wyandottes from one single pen, do you have only enough money to buy some berry plants?"

"The chickens have earned money, but I have needed it for day-to-day living," Bud said.

"Can Mr. and Mrs. Bennett help you at all?"

"They have a little more than four thousand dollars in the bank here at Haleyville, but that's all they have. They'll need it if anything goes wrong with either of them and I wondered if I could work my way through agriculture college?"

"You could, but I wouldn't consider earning all your expenses. At least, not at the beginning. Haven't you been able to sell any breeding stock from your Wyandottes?"

"No," Bud said. "That's one reason I want to go to college."

"What's your scholastic average?"

"B plus."

"Good, but not good enough for a scholarship even if there were enough of them for all able youngsters and if Haleyville Consolidated School received its just share. Allan, I don't want to be a killjoy, but you asked for my advice. Don't even think of college until you're able to finance at least your first semester. Then, if you show enough promise, the college will help you find ways to continue."

"How much will I need?" Bud asked.

"If you're careful, you should be able to get by with about seven hundred dollars. Perhaps even less."

"Seven hundred dollars!" Bud gasped.

"It isn't a million."

"It might as well be!"

"You can earn that much on summer jobs."

"Gramps has been sick. He can't spare me in summer."

"What will he do when you go to college?"

"It looks as though I'll be spared that worry," Bud said miserably. "If I need seven hundred dollars, I'm not going."

"You asked for my advice and I gave it, Allan, and I'd have rendered you no service if I hadn't been realistic," Mr. Demarest said gently. "If I had a magic wand to wave you into college with, believe me, I'd wave it. But I have no such thing. All you can do is to keep trying and never abandon hope."

Bud could say nothing, and finally Mr. Demarest said, "The bus has left. How will you get home?"

"I'll walk."

"I'll take you," Mr. Demarest said.

Bud rode in heartbroken silence up the snow-bordered highway. Mr. Demarest, who knew so much about so many things that Bud had almost believed he knew all about everything, hadn't been able to tell him how to get a college education. And so it was hopeless. Mr. Demarest drew up at the foot of the Bennetts' drive and put out his hand.

Mr. Demarest drove off and Bud tried to put a spring in his step and a tilt to his chin as he walked up the drive. The whole world, after all, had not fallen apart—just half of it. And Gramps was not only better but excited as a six-year-old over the prospect of hunting Old Yellowfoot tomorrow. Bud took off his overshoes, patted Shep and went into the kitchen.

Gram had just taken a tray of ginger cookies from the oven and put them on the table. Their odor permeated the whole kitchen. Gramps sat against the far wall happily oiling his rifle. Since Dr. Beardsley had given Gramps permission to go deer hunting this season, Gramps had been inspecting his rifle ten times a day. By now he had sighted it in so finely that he could almost drive nails with it at a hundred yards.

"Tomorrow's the day," Gramps said as Bud came in, "and I'm betting Old Yellowfoot will be hanging out in Dockerty's Swamp. You'd best get your own rifle in working order."

Bud said, "I already have."

Gram was more observant. "You're late, Allan," she said.

"I stayed to talk with Mr. Demarest," Bud said, in what he hoped was a casual tone. "He brought me home."

"What's the trouble?" she said, and Gramps looked up sharply.

"There's no trouble," Bud said.

"You can tell me, Allan. We're here to help you."

"If you're in a jam, Bud, we're on your side," Gramps said. "What'd you do? Sock the principal?"

"Honestly there's no trouble," Bud said. "Mr. Demarest and I talked about agriculture college."

"How nice," Gram said. "Every one of our boys and girls has gone to college. Now the twelfth will go, too."

"No he won't," Bud said. "Mr. Demarest said I hardly need a degree in agriculture if I'm going to stay here and take over Bennett's Farm. He said I can learn what I must know about poultry husbandry and berry culture as I go along."

"You're a right handy young feller at a lot of things," Gramps said. "But you're 'bout the poorest liar I ever laid eyes on. Joe Demarest never told you that."

"Well," Bud stammered, "not exactly. We had quite a talk."

"About what?"

"College."

"You make nine times as many circles as Old Yellowfoot with fifteen hunters hot on his tail," Gramps said. "He told you to go to college, didn't he?"

"Yes," Bud admitted. "But I'm not going."

"Why not?"

"I don't want to waste that much time. I can pick up what I must know as I go along."

"That is about the foolishest notion I ever heard," Gramps declared. "In my time I've met lots of men who didn't know enough, but offhand I can't remember any who knew too much. Sure you're going. Maybe you can't live like a millionaire's son on what we got in the bank, but you can get through."

"I can't take your money!" Bud blurted.

"Pooh," Gram sniffed. "What's money for? Of course you'll take it and we'll be mighty proud to have a college graduate running Bennett's Farm. Won't we,

158

Delbert?"

"Yeah," said Gramps who had begun to oil his rifle again. "Now you'd best get out of your school duds. I fed and bedded your hifalutin' chickens though I'm sort of uneasy around that one high-steppin' rooster. He's got so much blue blood that most any time at all I expect him to whip out one of those fancy glasses on sticks. That rooster sure ought to have one. He figures I'm not fit to be in the same chicken house with him. You beat it along now, Bud. I didn't milk the cows."

"Take a couple of cookies with you," Gram said.

Bud grabbed a handful of cookies and went up to his room. As he went about changing into work clothes, Bud kept his jaws clamped tightly. Gram and Gramps were wonderful, but they were so hopelessly out of touch with the world that they understood neither the value of money nor why Bud couldn't take the savings they had accumulated almost penny by penny over nearly half a century. They still added to it, but still almost penny by penny, and there was not even a possibility of sudden wealth. Anyway, Bud said to himself, he had another year of high school before he could even hope to enter college. Perhaps something would turn up before then. But in his heart he knew nothing would and he decided to say no more about college.

There was no point in arguing with Gram and Gramps.

As Bud milked the cows, took care of the stock and ate the evening meal with Gram and Gramps, he all but forgot his lost hope for a college education. Tomorrow's hunt for Old Yellowfoot was too exciting for him to brood over what could not be helped.

The tinny clatter of his alarm clock jarred him out of deep sleep the next morning well before the usual time. Bud shut the alarm off, leaped to the floor, and padded across it to revel for a moment in the frigid blast that blew in his open window. With snow on the ground and weather cold enough to keep it from melting without being too cold for comfort, it was a perfect day for hunting deer.

When he returned to the kitchen after doing the morning chores, Gram was making pancakes and cooking sausage and Gramps was sitting in a chair. "Why didn't you call me?" he growled. "We'd have been in the woods sooner if I'd helped with the chores."

"Now don't be grouchy," Gram said. "Old Yellowfoot's been roaming about Bennett's Woods for a good many years. I think he'll last another fifteen minutes."

"A body would figure I'm a crippled old woman," Gramps said. "Maybe you should ought to wrap me up in cotton and put me to bed so I won't get scratched or something. Pah! I never did see the beat of such a business!"

"If you're feeling as mad as all that," Gram said sharply, "you won't have to shoot Old Yellowfoot. Just bite him and he'll die from hydrophobia."

Bud giggled and Gramps couldn't help chuckling.

"Of all the dang fools in the world, people are the dangdest," he said. "I put myself in mind of Charley Holan, who said he'd be the happiest man in Dishnoe County if he just had a good brood sow. He got the sow and then he needed a place to keep it. So he said he'd be the happiest man ever if he had a place to keep it. He got one and found he needed a boar. Charley got the boar and first thing you know he was overrun with pigs. They did poorly that year, it didn't even pay to haul 'em to market. So Charley says he'd be the happiest man in Dishnoe County if he'd never even seen a pig. And this is the first season in the past three I've ever been able to hunt Old Yellowfoot. We'll tag him 'fore the season ends, Bud."

"I hope so, Gramps," Bud said.

"Dig in. It takes a pile of Mother's pancakes and a heap of sausage to see a man through a day in the deer woods."

After breakfast they stepped into the cold predawn

blackness. Shep, tied as usual while deer season was in swing, came to the end of his rope, whined, pressed his nose against their hands and pleaded as usual to be taken along.

Gramps stopped just inside Bennett's Woods, almost in sight of the barn. It was still too dark to shoot, but they often saw deer from the barn and they could expect to see deer from now on. It was true that Old Yellowfoot had never been seen so near the farm but that was no sign he never would be.

They went on as soon as they were able to sight clearly on a target a hundred yards away. Their jackets were tightly buttoned and their earmuffs pulled down against the frosty air. A doe faded across the trail like a gray ghost, leaving sharply imprinted tracks in the snow. A little farther on they saw a small buck. Then a doe and fawn ran wildly through the woods, and Gramps halted in his tracks.

Bud stared. Since he had come to Bennett's Farm he had seen many deer, and many of them had been running. But he had never seen any of them run like this.

"That pair's scared," Gramps said. "In all my born days I haven't seen ten deer run that fast, and the last one had wolves on its trail."

"Could wolves be chasing these?" Bud asked.

Gramps shook his head. "As far as I know, there hasn't been a wolf in Bennett's Woods for twenty-six years. Me and Eli Dockstader got the last one, and there's nothing else I can recall offhand that could start a couple of deer running that way and keep 'em running. Still, it has to be something."

Off in the distance, rifles began to crack as hunters started sighting and shooting at deer. Gramps and Bud paid no attention, for if other hunters could see them, they must be ordinary deer.

When they reached Dockerty's Swamp, where Gramps thought they might find Old Yellowfoot, Bud said, "Let me go down and track him through, Gramps, and you take it easy."

"Poof!" the old man said. "If Old Yellowfoot's in there, there's just one man got a chance of putting him out and that's me. Doc Beardsley said I could come deer hunting, didn't he? 'Sides, did you ever know a deer hunter—I'm talking of deer hunters and not deer chasers—who took it anything 'cept easy? The slower you go, the more deer you see."

"That's so," Bud admitted.

"Kite round and get on your stand," Gramps ordered. "I'll be through by and by."

He disappeared and Bud circled the swamp to the

brush-grown knoll that deer chose as an escape route when they were driven out of Dockety's Swamp. Rifles, some of them close and some distant, cracked at sporadic intervals as other hunters continued to find and shoot at deer. Bud waited quietly, with a couple of chickadees that were sitting nearby on a sprig of rhododendron for company.

Before long he saw something move down the slope. Bud stiffened, ready to shoot. It could only be a deer. But at the moment it was too far away and too well hidden by brush for him to tell what kind of a deer. Then it came on up the slope and Bud saw that it was a very good ten-point buck, but he refrained from shooting. The ten point was a nice trophy but he was not Old Yellowfoot.

Then nine does came by in no hurry, but without lingering as they walked through the sheltering brush into the forest beyond. They were followed by two smaller bucks, and then by another doe. Two and a half hours after Bud had taken up his stand, Gramps reappeared. Bud saw with relief that the old man did not look tired or even winded. Doc Beardsley had known what he was talking about when he had said Gramps was able to hunt deer this season.

"There were plenty of deer in the swamp, but Old

Yellowfoot wasn't among 'em," Gramps said. "We'll try Dozey Thicket."

But Old Yellowfoot was not in Dozey Thicket or Hooper Valley or Cutter's Slashing or Wakefoot Hollow. Nor did they find Old Yellowfoot the next day, although they saw at least three bucks with imposing racks of antlers.

On Monday Bud had to return to school and Gramps hunted alone. All week long he had no success, but when Bud came home Friday, Gramps was waiting for him in the kitchen. There was an air of triumph about him and a hunter's gleam in his eye.

"Found him, Bud," he said as soon as Bud came through the door.

"No!"

"Sure 'nough did! He's gone plumb out of Bennett's Woods into that footy little thicket above Joe Crozier's place. I saw his track where he came to the top of the hill and went back again, but I didn't hunt him 'cause I was afraid I might spook him. But two of us can get him right where he is."

Saturday morning, Bud and Gramps waited for dawn on the ridge overlooking Joe Crozier's thicket. When daylight came, they sighted their rifles on a rock about a hundred yards away, and for a moment neither spoke.

Crozier's thicket had at one time been a fine stand of hardwoods. Joe Crozier's father had cut the larger trees and buzzed them up for firewood, and the thicket had grown back to spindly young saplings. It was just the place a wise buck like Old Yellowfoot would choose as a refuge during hunting season, for nobody would ever think of looking for him there. But it was also a place where experienced hunters who did stumble onto his refuge would surely kill him.

"Let's go down," Gramps said softly.

Side by side they descended the hill, but when they were still forty yards from Crozier's thicket, they stopped. There was a patch of dark gray there that might have been a protruding knob of a tree or a boulder, but it wasn't. Old Yellowfoot, who knew the odds but was not about to give up, began to try to sneak away.

He was as huge as ever and he had lost none of his cunning. But his left antler was now only a single straight spike and his right one a snarled welter of many points.

Bud almost cried with disappointment, for he knew how Gramps had dreamed of the royal trophy Old Yellowfoot's antlers would make. And now he had overtaken Old Yellowfoot only to find him in his decadence. Never again would Old Yellowfoot be a worth-while trophy for anyone. He had succumbed to age.

As Bud was about to speak to Gramps, the old man said serenely, "Nature got to him before we could and I reckon that's as it should be. He was just a little too good to hang on anybody's wall. Let's go see Mother."

A WEEK LATER, BUD AND GRAMPS WENT INTO BEN-nett's Woods to bring out a load of firewood. Bud drove the team, Gramps sat on the bobsled seat beside him and Shep tagged amiably behind. They were half a mile from the farmhouse when the horses stopped of their own accord and raised their heads to stare. Looking in the same direction, Bud saw the black buck.

More darkly colored than any other deer Bud had ever seen, the buck was standing rigidly still in a little opening between two clusters of stunted hemlocks. His antlers had become magnificent. The black buck's head was high, and his eyes wary and his nostrils questing. A second later he glided out of sight into the nearest hemlocks.

For a moment Bud and Gramps sat enthralled, scarcely believing what they had seen. Then Gramps sighed and said, "Nothing's ever really lost, Bud. That's as good a head as Old Yellowfoot ever carried. Next year we'll hunt the black buck."

chapter 10

THE SPRING SUN WAS warm on Bud's back as he bent over the freshly tilled garden plot. He plucked a single strawberry plant from the tray beside him, trimmed off a precise third of its roots with a pair of Gram's old scissors and cut off a broken leaf. Then he scooped out a hole big enough to let the remaining roots fan out. Strawberries must be planted not too deep and not too shallow, Mr. Demarest had said, but at exactly the right depth. Although there were several systems for establishing a strawberry bed, Mr. Demarest favored starting with the plants one foot apart in rows three feet apart. This made for large fruit, he said; and, once the plants had matured so that they formed a matted row eighteen inches or two feet wide, there would still be enough space to weed, mulch and cultivate them.

The strawberry plant firmly imbedded, Bud was using a twelve-inch stick to measure the distance to the next one when Gramps came up behind him and said, "You're a thirty-second of an inch off."

Bud looked around and grinned. Gramps had been caustic when Bud had asked him if he could rent a patch of ground for a strawberry bed. According to Gramps, the farm was used to good old-fashioned crops like potatoes, corn, beans and oats, and wasn't likely to take kindly to anything so newfangled as strawberries. Anyhow, Gramps had wanted to know, who in his right mind would think of planting culti-vated berries when you could go out in the fields and pick all the wild ones you wanted?

When Gram had reminded Gramps of the high price Pat Haley paid for cultivated berries, Gramps had replied that it was not his fault if fools and their money were soon parted. But if Bud wanted a straw-berry patch, and if he wanted to do all the work of plowing and preparing the plot himself, he wouldn't stop him. But he couldn't in all conscience charge him rent because, as anybody could see, there would never be any profits. And if there were any, he could always reconsider.

Gramps became even more eloquent when Bud said that he wanted to plant a raspberry and a blackberry patch as well as soon as he had the money to buy plants. There were hundreds of raspberry tangles and blackberry thickets in Bennett's Woods, Gramps had pointed out, and anyone too lazy to go out in the woods and pick his own raspberries or blackberries would never earn enough money to buy cultivated ones. What was the world coming to, anyhow? In his day they had taught common sense instead of foolishness in school.

But actually the old man was delighted because Bud wanted to stay on and eventually take over Bennett's Farm. Bud knew that secretly Gramps approved of the new venture and was being caustic because he didn't want to inflate Bud's ego. Gramps was too realistic to stand in the way of young blood and young ideas. He knew that it is inevitable for the young to take over when the old can no longer carry on—just as Old Yellowfoot had relinquished his crown to the black buck. Bud had already proved that purebred chickens would outproduce a mongrel flock, and Gramps had replaced his flock with White Wyandottes like Bud's. Although Gramps had never thought of growing cultivated berries, he saw its potential and looked on Bud's new venture as a forward step that the young, not the old, should take.

"How many of those plants you got, Bud?" Gramps asked as he inspected the row Bud had planted so far.

"Two hundred."

"What'd you pay for 'em?"

"Forty dollars."

Gramps whistled. "Twenty cents each for those piddling little plants?"

"I could have had good plants for less," Bud said, "but Mr. Demarest recommended these. They're bred especially for this climate and soil, and they're ever-bearing."

Gramps chuckled. "I mind the time Mother and me picked your first pen of chickens. We might have had some real good ones for half what yours cost. But Mother said 'Delbert Bennett! If we're going to give that boy chickens for Christmas, let's give him the best or none!' Now danged if they ain't running all over the farm."

"Are you sorry?" Bud queried.

"Oh, I could have done the same thing," Gramps said casually. "Matter of fact, I was thinking about it. Will say, though, that the more you put in at the beginning the more you're like to take out at the end, and Joe Demarest usually knows what he's talking about. I expect your berries will do right well if drought don't get 'em, or flood rains don't wash 'em out, or somebody's cattle don't trample 'em, or any of a couple dozen other things don't happen to 'em."

Gramps grinned, and then he said, "How long do you figure on being busy, Bud?"

"I'm not sure," Bud said. "I may be busy all morning." Two hundred strawberry plants were not so many, but Mr. Demarest always made much of the importance of doing things the right way, and this was the first time Bud had done anything like this on his own. He was determined to plant them properly even if it took all day.

"Shucks," Gramps said. "I got me another trout spotted."

Bud glanced up eagerly. "You have?"

"Sure have," Gramps said. "He lives two pools below the one where we saw the otter playing. He ain't as big as Old Shark, but he's big enough."

At first Bud was about to heel in the remaining

strawberry plants and finish the next day. Then he thought again. The plants had cost almost all the money he had been able to save and, far more important, he had set out to accomplish something. Gramps was practically retired now and he could do about what he pleased. But Bud couldn't.

"I'd like to, Gramps," he said reluctantly, "but I've got to get the rest of these planted."

There was a brief silence before Gramps said, "Remember when we finally caught up with Old Yellowfoot but didn't shoot him because his antlers were no longer worth it? And remember the black buck we ran across while we were fetching a load of wood a while back?

"The more I think about him, the more I think he has a better rack of antlers than Old Yellowfoot ever had. I got to get me one really good head 'fore I hang up my rifle, and that's the one. We'll line our sights on him next season sure, Bud."

Bud kept his head down so Gramps could not see his face. He could not harm the black buck, but neither could he hurt Gramps. He had hoped the old man would forget the black buck, but from the beginning he had known that was a forlorn hope.

Gramps forgot nothing connected with Bennett's Woods.

"What did you say, Bud?" Gramps asked.

"Why, sure we'll go deer hunting."

Gramps said, "We'll do more than that. We'll hunt the black buck and we'll get him. Well, seeing that you're so all-fired busy, I might as well start puttering about myself. Maybe I can even make Mother think I'm working for a change."

The old man left, and Shep rose from the grass in which he had been lying down to tag behind him. All at once Bud felt that he knew why he wanted to stay on Bennett's Farm. Even though few people can write great poetry, compose deathless music, paint immortal pictures, the creative urge could find its expression on the farm. Gram in her flawless kitchen, Gramps among his crops or in the woods and fields he loved so dearly and understood so well, were truly creative and therefore truly happy. So was Mr. Demarest, the underpaid, overworked agriculture teacher at Haleyville High.

Bud did not understand the whys and wherefores, but he knew that he wouldn't change places with anyone on this bright spring day. Planting strawberries might not be the ultimate in human achievement, but

Bud knew that it suited him.

Then he frowned. Before preparing his strawberry bed, he had read all the books he could find on the subject and had talked at length with Mr. Demarest. According to the directions, the plants had to be set out precisely one foot apart in rows three feet apart. It was all very well to go by the book, but conditions vary even from field to field, and Bud realized that he did not know enough to adapt the method of planting to make it ideal for the special conditions of his strawberry bed. The more he knew about farming, the more keenly he felt his ignorance. But he had almost abandoned his dream of getting a degree in agriculture. Even so he was determined to learn anyhow. If he couldn't go to college, he could at least get the textbooks used there and teach himself. That would be hard, but if it was the only way, he would do it. He loved Bennett's Farm too much not to give it the attention it deserved.

Shep wandered back from wherever he had left Gramps and threw himself down in the grass to watch Bud, who looked at him affectionately. Shep had been his first friend when he came to Bennett's Farm and his true friend since. Shep had no pedigree, but a loving heart, and unswerving loyalty counted for a great deal, too.

"Only half a dozen more, Shep," Bud said. "Then I'll water them and we're through."

Shep wagged his tail lazily and grinned with his panting jaws. When Bud finished planting, Shep paced alongside him as he went to the barn for the hose.

Bud had chosen his strawberry patch partly for its location, for it caught the morning sun but was sheltered by a grassy knoll from the blazing heat of the midsummer afternoon sun. Wild strawberries had grown there plentifully, too, and it was near enough to the barn so that the farm's hundred-and-fifty-foot hose could be attached to the barn spigot and reach all corners of the bed.

The plants needed water now to help them overcome the shock of transplanting, and Bud watered them carefully, using a fine spray to keep from washing the loose soil away and at the same time giving each plant enough water to soak thoroughly both the roots of the plant and the earth about it. He had almost finished when Shep began to bark.

Bud looked around to see Sammy Toller, whose farm was a mile and a half north of Gramps', coming from the barn toward him. A small but tremendously energetic little man, Sammy was usually the epitome of good humor. Now his jaw was set, and his eyes smoldered and he did not even appear to notice the freshly planted berries.

"Is Delbert about?" Sammy asked.

"He's here somewhere, Mr. Toller," Bud said. "I'll find him as soon as I've rolled up this hose."

"Can you leave the hose for now?" Sammy asked. "This is pretty important."

Shep trailed along as they walked back to the barn, and Bud shut off the water at the spigot. They found Gramps working the newly spaded family garden with a hand rake. He looked around and said amiably,

"Hi, Sammy."

" 'Lo, Delbert. Got a few minutes?"

"Sure thing. What's up?"

"I'd druther take you to my place so you can see for yourself."

"Can I go along?" Bud asked.

"Sure," Gramps said, "but scoot along and tell Mother where we're going."

After racing into the kitchen and back, Bud climbed into the cab of Sammy's pickup truck with Sammy and Gramps, Shep leaped into the rear. Sammy eased the truck down the drive into the road and turned north toward his own farm. Ordinarily Sammy was lo-

178

quacious but he said nothing as they jogged along.

Sammy's house was a mile from the highway and his closest neighbor was half a mile away, which made his one of the most isolated farms in the Haleyville district. Otherwise it was very much like the surrounding farms, with a substantial house and the usual barns and outbuildings. Chickens were wandering about and a little group of Shropshire sheep—Sammy was trying to build up a registered flock of them—was huddled together in a pen near the barn. As they drove up, Sammy's dog, a farm collie like Shep, acted as if he was about to exterminate them until Shep walked stiffly forward. Then the two dogs sniffed noses, wagged their tails and went off for a romp.

"We'll have to walk a mite," Sammy said, and he led them up a hill from which the forest had been cleared from only the lower two-thirds. There was a long-abandoned apple orchard about a hundred yards from where the forest began, and a crow in one of the trees cawed lazily as they approached.

After Sammy had led them around the orchard, Bud stopped in his tracks at the sight of eighteen sheep strewn over the field between the orchard and the forest. All of them were horribly bloated and mangled.

"I turned 'em out yesterday morning," Sammy said,

"and I sure never heard a thing to make me s'pose they were getting murdered. When they didn't come home last night I hunted 'em, and this is what I found 'bout an hour ago."

The two dogs trotted forward and sniffed at the first of the dead sheep. Neither gave any sign that anything was amiss. Gramps stood a moment, studying the dogs, and then he went to look at one of the sheep.

"Dog work," he said.

"How do you know?" Sammy said.

"Wolves kill clean and eat what they kill. They don't murder just for cussedness and they don't mangle. What's more, these were wild dogs."

"What makes you so all-fired sure?"

"Were you here all day yesterday, when those sheep must have been killed?"

"Yep."

"But you heard nothing?"

"Nary a whisper."

"Tame dogs you'd have heard. They haven't the sense to keep their mouths shut on a job like this. Wild ones know that the less noise they make, the longer they live."

Now Bud remembered the doe and fawn that he and Gramps had seen during the last deer season when he and Gramps had been hunting Old Yellowfoot. Gramps had said that something was chasing them. There must have been wild dogs in Bennett's Woods even then, and no wonder the doe and fawn had been running as though they were possessed.

"What can we do?" Sammy asked.

"Anything we try will take a heap of doing," Gramps said. "These wild dogs know more than the smartest trap-pinched fox you ever saw. Still, we'd best do all we can to stop 'em. Most of the time they hunt in the woods, but there's no telling when they'll come again or who they'll hit."

"How does a body go about stopping 'em?" Sammy asked.

"If it was most anything 'cept wild dogs I could tell you. A fox sticks pretty much to his own beat and habits. So does a deer, bear, cat or 'most anything else. But wild dogs haven't any pattern. The most we can do is, first of all, set traps. I doubt if it'll work 'cause the pack that killed these sheep haven't been back to eat off 'em. I don't think they'll decoy to bait either. We might bump into 'em by rambling round with deer rifles."

Sammy Toller said grimly, "Soon's I take you home, I aim to start rambling with my deer rifle."

Sammy took Bud, Gramps and Shep home and then roared back up the road at forty miles an hour, an unheard-of speed for Sammy. Gramps was serious and sober and Bud wondered. Dogs were dogs; did running wild make them so very different?

"Are these wild dogs really bad?" he asked Gramps.

"Didn't you see Sammy Toller's dead sheep?"

"Yes, but wasn't that unusual?"

"Not a bit. I'd rather face a pack of timber wolves than a bunch of wild dogs any day. Where a wolf will kite off and keep on kiting, a dog will plan. He'll run just far enough to get out of a man's sight. Then he'll figure some way to fool him and nine times out of ten he'll do it. Just a minute."

Gramps went to the telephone, and as soon as he had finished telling Pete Nolan, the game warden, about the wild dogs, the old man turned to Bud and said, "Let's you and me mosey out in the woods, and we'll pack rifles."

With Shep keeping pace, they sauntered into Bennett's Woods. A doe that was heavy with fawn crept off, but a strutting cock grouse scarcely bothered to move out of the way. Turkeys slunk away from their hidden nesting sites, and from a knoll a buck with grotesque knobs of antlers watched and stamped a threatening forefoot.

They found no sign of the pack in Bennett's Woods that day, but not long afterward Pete Nolan came upon six of the pack harrying one of Tommy Keeler's heifers and shot two of the wild dogs before the others fled. Jess Limley got another and Sammy Toller shot two when the pack had returned for another attack on his sheep. By the time the hunting season rolled around again, it was generally agreed that there were at least ten dogs in the pack and it was certain that they were still prowling the woods.

chapter   11

LEAVES CRISP WITH FROST
rustled beneath Bud's pacs as he strode on through
the woods. His shotgun was half raised, but his mind
was not on the grouse that, any moment now, might
rocket up from the copse of brush he was approaching.

He sighed. It had been a busy summer and not entirely a good one. There had been a good crop of
young chickens, but a mysterious malady had killed
a third of them. Neither he nor Gramps had been
able to discover what it was. Gramps thought the

trouble was that the White Wyandottes were less hardy than crossbreeds. Bud was sure Gramps was mistaken, although none of his books gave a clue as to what was wrong. More keenly than ever, Bud felt his lack of knowledge and the need to acquire more.

During the spring and summer he had not worried much about hunting for the black buck. Autumn and the deer season had seemed very far away then. But now the season was here, and Gramps' anticipation mounted daily.

Since school had reopened, Gramps had made as intensive a study of the black buck and his habits as he had of Old Yellowfoot and his. At least three times a week and sometimes more often, Gramps went into Bennett's Woods to observe the buck. By now, Gramps knew the buck's favorite haunts, his drinking places, when he liked to rest and when he foraged. Twice Gramps had been within rifle shot, by which the old man concluded that the black buck was not as cunning as Old Yellowfoot. Still, the black buck would be no easy game, and he had an even bigger rack than Old Yellowfoot's at its best. To hang that rack on the living-room wall would be the crowning achievement of Gramps' career as a hunter and fisherman. Between them, Gramps had made up his mind, he and Bud would hang it there.

It occurred to Bud there in the autumn woods that if Gramps became ill again, he wouldn't be able to go on hunting the black buck. Bud still felt that a bond existed between him and the black buck, that his destiny and the buck's hung on the same thread, so that Bud's good fortune in being at Bennett's Farm would end if anything happened to the buck. But Bud realized at once that he would rather face the end of the buck and of his own happiness than another of Gramps' attacks.

Just as he came to that conclusion, the grouse rose in a thunder of wings. Bud raised his gun and knew as he shot that the bird he was aiming at was out of range. Then he heard Gramps' gun boom twice and saw two grouse plummet into the leaves.

"Dreaming today?" Gramps called. "As Pete Henderson said to his boy, Ben, 'I've taught you all I know and you still don't know nothing.' That was as neat a straightaway shot as I ever saw."

"I wasn't ready."

"We'll teach a few grouse to wait until you are," Gramps said. "I swear to gosh, Bud, you act like you got a girl on your mind."

Gramps went forward to pick up his grouse. He

held them by the legs and their mottled plumage rippled in the faint breeze. Gramps, who had seen half a thousand grouse, looked for a moment at these two as though they were the first. Then he walked to and sat down on a mossy log.

"Guess I'm getting old," he remarked. "I doubt if I'll be hunting Bennett's Woods more than another forty or fifty years."

Bud said nothing as Gramps laid his grouse carefully in the leaves beside the log and ejected the two spent shells from his double-barreled twelve shotgun. The limit for grouse was four, but Gramps believed that two was enough for any hunter.

After they had sat together on the log for a while, Gramps said, "I ran across Old Yellowfoot day before yesterday and all he's got this year is two spikes. I swear he knows it, too, and that spikes ain't legal. Stood no more than twenty yards away, chewing his cud like any old cow and hardly giving me a second look. He'll be safe unless one of those trigger-happy hunters who'll shoot at anything runs across him, and I doubt if one of those can find him. He hasn't lost his brains just 'cause the rest of him started downhill."

"He's earned his right to peace."

" 'Peace' is a word with a lot of stretch, Bud. Take

people now. Some get it one way and some another, and some never get it. Heinrich Umberdehoven can't have any peace 'thout he's working, because only when he's working is there any hope of earning another dollar or two. Rudy Bursin, he don't have any peace unless he's loafing, and he'd rather be known as the Haleyville town bum than work. Sammy Toller never gets any peace and I don't know why unless it's 'cause he's always deviled by notions. When his sheep petered out, he figured to go in for cattle feeding. If that don't work, he'll try something else. If it does, he'll be fretted trying to make it bigger and better. Old Yellowfoot might have peace if by that you mean he's safe from hunters. But I think he'd rather be hunted."

"Why?"

"He's old, and the way he lives it ain't nice to get old. His bones will ache, he'll feel the cold, he'll have a rough time finding enough to eat in winter, and by and by he'll just naturally lay down and die. It won't be because he has to, but because his life will not be worth living any more. While he was being hunted he was in his prime, and he never gave a darn anyhow because he knew he could get away from any hunter. He did it for a good many years, and I think he got as much fun out of fooling hunters as they did out of hunting him."

For the first time it occurred to Bud that hunting could be a two-way street and that the hunted sometimes took as keen a delight in eluding their pursuers as the hunters in pursuing. "It makes sense," he said after he had thought it over.

"It is sense," Gramps said, " 'less you get some poor little scared thing too young to know what it's all about, and those you oughtn't to hunt anyhow. But I'm sort of glad we didn't get Old Yellowfoot."

"Why?"

"He had the biggest rack I ever saw and I figured it'd be the biggest I ever would see. But the black buck beats him, and it ain't right for one person to kill two big deer. One's a trophy but two's hoggishness. If you get the buck you want, and the black buck is the one I want, leave the next big one for somebody else."

A fuzzy caterpillar, driven by some unseasonal urge, started crawling up the log on which they were sitting. Gramps pointed at the caterpillar, which was black at both ends and brown between.

"We're in for some early bad weather," he said.

"How do you know?" Bud asked.

"The longest black's on the fore end of that caterpillar, and that always means the fore end of the winter will be long and hard."

Bud pondered this piece of information. Gramps' lore had proved valid so often in the past that Bud knew better than to dismiss what the old man was saying about caterpillars as so much local superstition. Shortly after Bud had come to the farm, Gramps had told him that, when swallows flew near the ground, a storm was in the making. Bud hadn't taken much stock in that until he learned in school that the low-pressure area that precedes a storm drives insects down near the earth and so the swallows follow them. Therefore, when swallows fly close to the ground, a storm does usually follow.

"You aim to get yourself a couple of grouse?" Gramps asked.

"I don't think so," Bud said.

"Something is chewing on you," Gramps said. "What is it?"

"Nothing," Bud said, turning his face away because he could not look at Gramps and tell an untruth.

"You ain't going to stop hunting?" Gramps asked.

"Two grouse are plenty for the three of us."

"I hope you don't feel like hanging fire when we

go after the black buck."

"I'll hunt him with you," Bud promised.

"Then we'll get him." Gramps seemed relieved. "Well, let's mosey home and see how Mother's doing."

IN HIS FIRST FREE PERIOD THE FOLLOWING MONDAY, Bud sat in the principal's outer office at Haleyville High School. After five minutes Mr. Thorne's secretary told him to go in. Bud, who had always been at ease with Mr. Thorne, was nervous.

"I'd like permission to be excused from school for as much of the deer season as necessary, sir," he said stiffly.

"Want to get yourself a buck, eh?"

"Well, partly."

"Do you think that hunting is more important than your academic career?"

"No, sir."

"Then what is it?"

"There's a big buck in Bennett's Woods," Bud blurted out. "Gramps—Mr. Bennett, that is—has always dreamed of killing just such a deer. It's sort of like a dream he's always had. Gramps had been sick and he isn't exactly young. No one can be sure he'll be able to hunt next deer season. He has to get the black buck this year. He thinks I can help him."

"In other words you want to stay out of school for an indefinite period to help Delbert Bennett get this buck. Well, I think it can be arranged." Then, before Bud could thank him, Mr. Thorne went on. "In fact, I think it will be a very important part of your education. You may not see what I mean now, but maybe you will later."

Gramps, who was splitting wood when Bud got home that afternoon, yelled "Hallelujah!" when he heard the good news and threw a stick of firewood in the air. "The black buck's as good as ours," he said.

NOT LONG AFTERWARD THE SCHOOL BUS WAS crawling up the highway behind the snowplow that was clearing four inches of new snow that had added itself to the four inches that had fallen yesterday. Bud was staring out the window, almost oblivious to

Goethe Shakespeare Umberdehoven who sat beside him as usual. He saw little since wind-blown sheets of snow obscured everything more than twenty yards from the highway, but he was thinking of the caterpillar that had crawled up the log when Gramps scored his double on grouse. Bud had been a little skeptical when Gramps had predicted a harsh, early winter from the caterpillar's markings, but now it looked as if they were in for the earliest and harshest winter in ten years.

When Get Umberdehoven asked if he was going deer hunting, Bud said "Yeah" without turning away from the window.

"You don't seem so excited about it."

"Why don't I?" Bud snapped.

"Always before when deer season came you couldn't hardly sit still. Now you act like you'd rather not go."

"Oh shut up!" Bud said. Then, feeling remorseful, he turned to face Get. "Are you going deer hunting?"

"Everybody goes the first day and we got to get a deer because if we do"—Bud waited for what he knew was coming next—"we can sell another pig."

"I'm going to stay out and hunt for as long as I want to," Bud said loftily. "I'll hunt the whole season if I feel like it."

"I wish I could," Get said. "School, it's hard for

me. But if I don't go, I fall behind, and if I fall behind . . ." He shrugged eloquently.

Bud thought of Mr. Thorne's saying that he thought it would be a very important part of Bud's education to hunt the black buck, but he still had no idea what Mr. Thorne really meant. There were a lot of things he did not understand, Bud decided as the bus stopped in front of the Bennetts' driveway.

"Good luck," he said to Get to make up for having snapped at him.

"Yeah," Get said listlessly.

Bud left the bus and made his way through the eight inches of fluffy snow that blanketed the driveway. The snow was loose and easy to plow through. But still it would either keep the more timid hunters out of the woods entirely or make them concentrate in the fringe areas so that there would be fewer hunters in the deep woods.

Shep came to meet him as Bud stomped the snow from his overshoes and took them off on the porch, and for a moment Bud wished he could change places with Shep, who wasn't allowed to go out into the deer woods during the season. Then he opened the door and went into the kitchen.

A heavenly smell from the loaves of freshly baked bread that Gram was tumbling out of baking pans filled every corner of the kitchen and overflowed into the nearby rooms. Gramps sat at the table fussing with some minor adjustment of his deer rifle.

"All set, Bud?" he said, grinning.

"All set."

"Good. Tomorrow we get on his tail! Give us four days together, just four days, and you and me'll tag that black buck."

Gram said, "Oh, Delbert. You'd think that buck was more important than the President of the United States."

"Right now, and as far as I'm concerned, he is, Mother. 'Sides, who'd want the President's head hanging on his setting-room wall?"

Gram appealed to Bud. "That's all he's been talking about, just that black buck. And if he's been over his rifle once today, he's been over it a hundred times."

"Got to have it right, Mother," Gramps said. "We'll get one chance and no more. If we miss when the chance comes, we'll have only ourselves to blame."

"After all this fuss and bother you'd just better get him," Gram said dryly. "There'll be no living with you the rest of the winter if you don't. I'd give you a slice of butter bread, Allan, except that it's still too hot."

"I'm not hungry," Bud said. "I'll change my clothes and do the chores."

"I'll give you a hand," Gramps offered.

"No, you stay right here."

Bud went to his room, glad to escape. If only a miracle would occur. If only the snow would melt and the leaves would appear and deer season would be over with the black buck still in Bennett's Woods. There would be no miracle, Bud knew. There was just one thing he could do if the black buck came in range— shoot straight. Gramps wanted the head to hang in the living room and Bud would do his best to see that it hung there. It made no difference whether he or Bud shot the buck, since they would be working as a team.

Bud lingered at the chores, and for one of the very few times since he had come to live with the Bennetts, he had almost no appetite for supper. Gram looked at him with concern, but Gramps was too excited to notice.

"He won't be in the hills, Bud, with this snow," Gramps was saying. "He and all the other deer with sense, which means all the other deer, will be down in the valley swamps and thickets. If this snow deepens, and I think it will, the deer will yard in for another week or ten days. Do you know where we'll find that black buck?"

"Where?" Bud tried to inject enthusiasm into his voice.

"Hagen's Flat or Dockerty's Swamp," Gramps said. "I'm putting my money on Dockerty's Swamp. Not in twenty years have I put a buck out of there that I wanted to shoot, but I never lost the feeling that that's where my real luck lies. Yep, we'll find the black buck in Dockerty's Swamp."

The next morning, fortified with one of Gram's substantial breakfasts, and each with one of her ample lunches in his hunting jacket, Gramps and Bud left the house with Gram's warning not to overdo ringing in their ears. Bud glanced at Shep, whose feelings were hurt because he was tied up so he couldn't follow them into the woods.

The day grew lighter slowly and from far off came an occasional rifle shot or volley of shots as hunters began to encounter deer. Bud had been right the day before in thinking that the snow would keep most of the hunters in easily accessible areas, for most of the shooting was going on near the main highway. There were almost no shots from the deep woods but, as Gramps had predicted, that was where the deer were.

First they saw a herd of fourteen does and fawns that had been driven down from the hills by the stormy weather. Then there was a buck, a ten point with a very respectable rack of antlers. Either Gramps or Bud could have shot him before he glided out of sight in a rhododendron thicket. Next they saw a herd of nine in which there were two bucks.

They parted at Dockerty's Swamp. Gramps went down to track through the swamp while Bud took his stand on a knoll up which any deer driven from the swamp would be sure to run. The snow had stopped falling, but heavy clouds lingered in the sky and it would begin again. Now and then Bud saw a deer flitting across one of the few open spaces in Dockerty's Swamp, and he knew that the swamp must be almost overrun by deer seeking a refuge from the snow. But no deer came up the slope and before long it was clear that they preferred to take their chance in the swamp rather than to go back into the hills.

Bud had been at his stand a little less than an hour when he saw a deer running easily in the open country at the far edge of the swamp. Even if it had not been black, Bud would have known from its mighty rack of antlers that it was the black buck.

Bud raced down the slope, stopping to whistle when he reached the edge of the swamp. Then, receiving no answer, he went a short distance into the swamp and whistled again. This time there was a reply, and Bud found Gramps leaning against a dead stub.

"What in tunket are you doing?" he said angrily. "You should know better than to leave a deer stand."

"He went out the other side!" Bud said.

"The black buck?"

"Yes!"

"Come on!"

Bud led to where he had seen the black buck disappear and Gramps looked once at the tracks.

"It's him," he said, "and danged if he hasn't outsmarted us. He figures he knows as much about snow as we do, and I reckon he's right. Anyhow, he's going back into the hills."

They began to climb, and the snow became deeper and the drifts more frequent. Two-thirds of the way up Hammerson's Hill, Gramps turned to Bud.

"Give me an hour and come through on the track."

After a timed sixty minutes, Bud went ahead, following the buck's tracks. Before long he found Gramps, who had made a wide circle, standing beside a huge boulder. The tracks of the black buck, who had slowed from a run to a walk, still led on.

"I thought he came through here and he did," Gramps said. "But he came maybe ten minutes 'fore I got here. Ha! He thinks he's outsmarted us by taking to the hills, but could be he's tricked himself."

"How has he tricked himself?" Bud asked.

"Longer shooting," Gramps explained to Bud. "If we find where he's dipped into a gully, we have a good chance of catching him going up the other side."

They followed the tracks until two hours before dark. Whenever they came too near for comfort, the black buck would run a little way, but most of the time he was satisfied to walk. Then they found that he had given a mighty leap a full twenty feet to one side of his line of travel and begun to run continuously. The tracks of four wild dogs came from the opposite direction and joined those of the black buck where he had veered off.

Not speaking to save his breath for speed, Gramps followed the tracks. It was almost dark when he and Bud came to a place where the tracks separated, with the wild dogs' going off in one direction and the buck's in another.

"They smelled us coming and kited off," Gramps said. "But they'll be back.

"We'll start earlier tomorrow, Bud," the old man said as they turned to go home.

chapter 12

THE NEXT MORNING, WHEN Gramps and Bud returned to the black buck's track, the light was too dim for shooting and even for adequate tracking. A brisk little wind sent snow devils whirling before it, and the wind had blown most of the night, reducing the sharply imprinted tracks the black buck had left the day before to shallow depressions in the snow. The clouds were darker than yesterday and snow drifted down from them and mingled with the snow devils.

The valley below them looked as black as though it

was still midnight there, and above it, where Gramps and Bud were standing, the snow glowed weirdly in the pale light. Bud shivered, but he was grateful, too, for the very elements seemed to have conspired to save the fleeing black buck. Even Gramps couldn't hope to win against such odds as these.

Bud grew more and more uneasy as he stood there helplessly, not knowing what to do. Gramps seemed baffled, too, reluctant either to go on or to turn back. The old man raised his rifle, sighted at the black trunk of a birch tree about fifty yards away and then lowered his rifle uncertainly.

"He could be thirty yards away and the size of an elephant, and I still couldn't get my sights on him," Gramps said quietly. "That's what comes of selling a wise old buck short. He knew what he was doing when he came into the hills. He figured we were after him down in the swamp and was sure of it when we got on his tail. But he also knew there'd be more snow and he counted on it to cover his tracks."

"He's wise, all right," Bud said with secret elation. Yesterday he had seen nothing except doom for the black buck. But the buck had a wild wisdom all his own, and thanks to that and to the falling snow, he had escaped his pursuers. If his tracks were covered up by the snow, he might still live to reign once more in Bennett's Woods.

"We'll have to do our best anyhow," Gramps said. "If that pack finds him first, what's left won't be worth our carrying home."

Gramps' words were like an electric shock to Bud. He had thought of the pack and its pursuit of the buck, but it had not occurred to him that the wild dogs were competing with him and Gramps on equal terms. At the thought of the black buck as a piece of meat that happened to be charged with life, a prize contested for by Gramps and a pack of wild dogs, Bud could hardly keep from retching. He felt as if he had been swept back to the grim, loveless world he had known before he had come to the Bennetts'.

"I think you're right," Bud finally managed to answer.

"Let's get moving, then," Gramps said, and started off in the semidarkness with Bud behind him.

The buck had continued to run, twenty feet to the leap, even after the dogs had finally left his tracks the afternoon before. But the snow had shifted so much during the night that the places where he had landed were now so vaguely defined that Gramps and Bud's pace was agonizingly slow. They must go faster than this, Bud thought as he reached down for a handful of snow to cool his burning mouth. If it would mean the end of his good fortune if Gramps killed the buck, it would be even worse if the wild dogs killed him, for then Gramps' dream would be destroyed, too.

Restraining an impulse to rush past Gramps and find the black buck in a burst of speed, Bud began to watch Gramps and he grew less desperate as he saw the old man in action. The sullen light was too dim to see from one set of the black buck's tracks to the next, but Gramps never failed to know in which direction the buck had leaped. Gramps seemed to be thinking not as Delbert Bennett but as the black buck himself.

Perhaps the black buck enjoyed matching wits with hunters just as Old Yellowfoot seemed to, perhaps because he, too, was sure he could escape them. But wild dogs were different. The black buck had never run as far or as wildly with Gramps and Bud following him as he had even after the wild pack had stopped following. Plainly he knew what wild dogs could do and he was terrified.

The night lifted so slowly that its rise was almost imperceptible, and when dawn finally came, the clouds remained so dark that it did not seem to be day at all. But when he sighted on a tree about three hundred yards away and could see a knothole over the sights, Bud knew there was at least shooting light.

They were about a mile and a half from where they had returned to track the black buck. Where the tracks dipped into a gully whose only growth was wind-whipped aspens, the buck had slowed from a frantic run to a fast walk. Now that they were closer together and the light was stronger, the tracks were easier to follow. They turned straight up the gully toward the top of the hill.

Gramps halted and Bud stopped behind him without speaking. Bud's desperate urge to hurry was gone, for by now he knew better than to try to do in haste what had to be done slowly. Gramps had performed a miracle in bringing them this far, and Bud realized that such mastery of the wilds was the result of love for wild places and wild things as well as skill and the desire to conquer.

Then Gramps spoke, "He knows nothing's on his track any more and he thinks he's safe for a while. He's heading toward that patch of hemlocks on top of the hill because he's been pushed hard and needs a rest, and he can rest safely there. He's working back in the direction of the farm because there'll be more snow and he might have to get out of the hills in a hurry; he can do it by going down any of those deep gullys. But he knows those critters as well as I do, and he's going to be a mighty spooky buck until he's shaken that pack. He never was much afraid of us. But he's afraid of them."

"Will the dogs be back?" Bud's voice shook.

Gramps said grimly, "If they don't come, it's the first pack ever got on game and left it. They can't have that buck. I've marked him. Come on."

Leaving the tracks of the black buck, Gramps went straight across the gully, fought halfway through a thigh-deep drift and halted. Bud looked up in alarm, but there wasn't the terrible wheezing and the anguished fight for breath that there had been when Gramps suffered his attacks. His face was streaked with perspiration but its color was normal.

He had only stopped to rest, and after a moment he broke through the drift and quartered up the slope. Bud felt uneasily that he ought to be taking his turn breaking trail, but he knew better than to offer. It was Gramps' hunt and the buck was Gramps' prize. And only Gramps knew what to do.

It was hard to imagine these hills as they were in the full bloom of summer, when anxious does hovered there near spotted fawns hidden in thickets and summer-sluggish bucks, their antlers velvet-sheathed, moved out of the way as placidly as grazing cattle. In the summer, too, grouse and wild turkeys brought their downy young to feed there.

Now in the stormy depths of winter the hills looked like a desert of snow, although not all the wild life had fled. Cottontail rabbits huddled in their burrows and snowshoe hares crept about in the thickets. No doubt foxes and weasels were sheltering there from the storm and probably a few grouse and turkeys were still on the hills, too. But not even the track of a mouse could be seen on the virgin snow.

Bud glanced toward the valley and could see only a part of the way down the slope through the falling snow. There was life in abundance down there and for a moment he wished he were out of these hills where there seemed to be nothing but snow and a grim determination to end the black buck's life.

After Gramps had stopped to rest two more times, they broke over the crest of the hill. They traveled faster now, for although the snow was as deep as ever, the going was downhill. It was like coming out of the desert into an oasis when a grove of hemlocks loomed ahead. The hemlocks were partly covered with snow but their green needles were visible. They looked like Christmas trees decorated with great puffs of cotton.

Gramps entered the hemlocks very slowly, with his rifle half raised, and Bud almost hoped they would find the black buck in the grove and put an end to this almost unbearable uncertainty. But all they found, deep in the hemlocks, was a bed in which the weary buck had finally lain down. Apparently he had left it shortly before Gramps and Bud had returned to following his tracks that morning, for very little snow covered the tracks leading away.

When they came to the bed, Gramps stopped and said to Bud, "He's going to have himself a feed of beech nuts. Then he'll mosey down the hilltop to see if anything is on his trail. If he finds nothing, pretty soon he'll go back to the valley. He's afraid of this snow."

They came to a grove of gray-trunked beech trees so massive that they seemed impregnable to the wind and storm. Gramps and Bud were still a hundred yards away when they saw a pile of leaves freshly pawed through the snow and knew that the buck had been scraping for beech nuts. These tiny nuts came down like hail when the first frost opened their green pods, and there had been a great harvest of them that year.

Swiftly Gramps approached the place where the buck had been pawing, for the giant beech trees were widely separated and there was no brush to obscure the view. If the black buck was in the grove, they would see him. When they came to the scraped leaves, Gramps stopped again.

From where he stood the tracks of the wild dogs could be seen leading out of the beech grove and joining those of the black buck.

Gramps made a sound that was half a gasp and half a growl, and without looking back, began to move with giant strides along the mingled tracks. Bud hung back for a second. He had hunted and fished with Gramps hundreds of times, but he had never seen him react this way. Usually Gramps approached his quarry eagerly, but with a kind of reverence, too. Now Gramps seemed to have become a ferocious killer for whom the game was no longer a sport. Bud could only follow Gramps numbly, but it seemed to him that it had only become a question of whether Gramps or the wild dogs would kill the black buck first.

The buck was again making great leaps as the pack coursed him. Bud did not dare talk to Gramps, but he knew that no deer could maintain such a furious pace for long. And the longer-winded wild dogs could go on indefinitely.

Two miles after the pack had taken up the chase again, Gramps and Bud came upon the place where the dogs had first caught up with their quarry, and the trampled snow made it easy to reconstruct the scene. Pressed to his limit, the black buck had backed his haunches against a tangled windfall and waited with lowered antlers as the pack came on. The dogs had rushed and feinted, hoping to draw the buck out and make him expose his vulnerable flanks and hocks.

"Look!" Bud said, when he saw a patch of blood thinly covered by new snow.

"That ain't the black buck's blood," Gramps said. "If it was he never would have got out of here alive. He's hooked one of the dogs. They're not as anxious as they were."

It was true, Bud decided as he and Gramps raced on. The buck was still running hard, but he was no longer taking the same mighty leaps. No doubt that was partly because he was tired, but he had also taught the pack to respect him. Although they could have closed in on him, they had held off for another two and a half miles.

Then, on the rim of a shallow gully, the dogs had come forward with a determined rush. But the buck had backed up against three small trees whose trunks formed a triangle and held them off. There was no blood here, but when the buck had left, his leaps had been very short.

"He ain't going much farther," Gramps said grimly. "And he'll try to get back into the valleys where the snow ain't as deep. Come on. Hagen's Flat's the place he'll head for."

Gramps left the trail to quarter down the slope. Bud followed, not sure whether this was the right tactic, but not daring to question it. Gramps led them back down the snowy lifeless slope, and they ran on and on until Bud was sure they would run out of this world and into the next. When they came to the near side of a valley that sloped downward, they saw the black buck at bay across the valley.

This time there was no shelter for his haunches, and his feet were no longer nimble as the pack rushed him. The dogs were as big as wolves and determined to kill their quarry without getting hurt themselves. Two of the four wild dogs lunged at the black buck's haunches. But when he whirled around to confront them, they danced away and the other two dogs rushed in.

Bud was looking on frozen with horror when the sudden, sharp crack of Gramps' rifle startled him out of his trance. It was too far for any marksman who had been running, and he missed. The dogs turned to run and Gramps shot again, missing this time, too.

For a short time the black buck stayed where he was. Then he turned to go on, but his steps were very slow and very tired. He stumbled and almost fell. When he came to a drift so deep that the snow reached his shoulders, he stopped, too exhausted to move. He gave no sign of fear when Gramps and Bud came up to him. There was a serenity and a dignity about him, as if, having done his best and fought his hardest, he could do no more and was prepared for whatever he had to face.

As he looked at the buck there in the snowdrift, Bud thought of that summer day so long ago when the black buck had been a tiny fawn in his arms. The fawn had given Bud the courage to face life during those first days at Bennett's Farm and now what Bud had learned then was reconfirmed in the grown buck's quiet resignation to whatever fate had in store for him. Bud knew that he could fondle the buck now if he wanted to. The buck had no strength left to resist and his great antlers were as useless as those on the mounted head in the Bennetts' living room.

Then there was a click as Gramps slipped the catch

213

of his rifle from safe to fire. Gramps had his prize. The black buck was less than two yards away from him, and he couldn't miss. Bud waited for a shot, but none came.

"Kite down to the barn and fetch the toboggan and a good strong hank of rope, Bud," Gramps said finally. "I'll wait here and see if those critters come back. I hope they do. But even if they don't, now that we know where they are, we'll get 'em on this snow."

OUTSIDE THE WIND HOWLED AND THE SNOW SWEPT down. But the kitchen stove radiated warmth to every corner of the room. It even seemed to warm his heart, Bud thought, although he knew that couldn't be.

"You're sure he'll be all right?" he asked Gramps.

"Dead sure," Gramps said. "He couldn't even wiggle when we tied him on the toboggan, but he'll be full of beans in a few days. Time deer season ends, he'll have enough hay and grain in him so he'll be able to make his way back into Bennett's Woods." Gramps chuckled. "You 'n' me will just open that box stall and watch him kite out."

214

"Aren't you sorry?" Bud asked.

"Heck no," Gramps said. "He'll carry a bigger rack than ever next year, and it'll be bigger still the year after."